Coffee Mystery and Magic
A Prequel to
A Very Crafty Christmas
Misty Vale Cozy Mystery Book
1

Sarah Lewin © 2025

Coffee Mystery and Magic

First edition July 2025

ISBN 978-1-7637430-5-2 (ebook)

978-1-7642454-1-8 (Paperback)

www.sarahlewin.com[1]

---

1. http://www.sarahlewin.com

Chapter One

The letter was addressed to *Freida Everly*. I turned the envelope over to the back, gingerly, as if it might hurt me. I used that name such a long time ago. I'd also used *Martha Lovelace,* and *Eliza Vane.* More recently I'd settled for a more mundane monika – *Hannah White,* and occasionally the name I had been provided with at birth – *Jane Fairweather.*

A flash of purple and emerald green landed on the kitchen bench in front of me. "Whatcha got there?" Mystara, my miniature dragon statue with with glowing runes etched into its scales nudged his face up to the envelope. An old soul, with an ancient magic, he'd found me only a couple of years ago, choosing to occasionally keep me company on my travels.

I held the envelope so Mystara could see better. The rear of the envelope didn't reveal any clues as to the sender. "I'm not sure. It's addressed to Freida, and I haven't been her for years. Remember when I was a private investigator in that tiny room in London? Can you tell who wrote it and why?"

Mystara rolled his tiny dark blue eyes. "I could, but why don't you just open it?"

I cast my mind back to when I was Freida. Most of my clients sought confirmation of cheating spouses wanted me to find missing family members. The millionaires, with their endless pockets, determined for me to persist until I solved their mysteries, were willing to throw any amount of money at me, to find their runaway child, cripple an adversary, or help facilitate a business takeover. "I don't want to. I've left that part of my life behind."

Little puffs of light fluttered to the kitchen bench as Mystara stretched his wings. "You're worried it might be about a case you couldn't solve, or that didn't end well," he said knowingly. He read me as well as I read others – and I'd developed that skill over many years. "That guy who yelled at you, because his wife left him and refused to return home, or that vicious criminal – the reason why you changed your name and moved here," he suggested helpfully.

I held my hand out, and Mystara hopped up, his little talons tickling my skin. "It could be either, or someone else. I've lived in so many cities and with different names. It's weird, with all the moves and change, I've no emotional attachment to my names, or any building or city where I've lived." I sighed. No one mourned me as Freida, Eliza, Martha, Hannah, or Jane. "I moved here to be as far away from that life as I could get..."

Mystara's blue eyes bored into mine, I blinked first. "I'm not being melancholy. You know this is just somewhere to live and work." Travelling light, a suitcase of clothes and a small box of memories from my childhood, were the only items I carried with me halfway around the world. Each time I found an apartment in a city I rarely bothered to decorate. The tools of my trade were my laptop, a notepad and a pen. Whenever things got a little crazy, I moved on.

"I like this life, it's a little boring, but there's far less drama." As long as I kept to myself.

Mystara stepped off my hand. "You're calmer," he acknowledged, "With your emotions under control – mostly." He nudged my hand as the familiar tingling started in my fingers, indicating I was getting anxious.

I wiggled my fingers, aware that sparks would fly, confident nothing around me would catch fire. "It helps, retiring from my private investigator career. Working with indie authors, using my research and writing skills is less fraught with danger. Plus, I rarely have to leave the apartment." I agreed, squeezing my eyes shut tight as my stomach flip flopped. I forced myself to breathe in for the count of five, hold my breath for three and exhale, for the count of five. For years, this power of mine, caused all sorts of dramas, until I learnt how to control it.

I opened my eyes, focusing on my little friend, "I was only thirteen when weird things started happening. It freaked me out. I had no one to talk to, I thought there was something wrong with me. Sparks of electricity would shoot from my fingertips – short circuiting nearby electrical items. My energy would find ways to escape, knocking over expensive vases, breaking toys and other items. I remember trying to hide what was happening. Weird thunderstorms appeared whenever I was upset, which was a lot." Mystara nodded, little puffs of smoke wafted from his nostrils, encouraging me to verbalise, to release me anxiety. "I don't know if I inherited my skills from my parents – they never mentioned it."

"You found people like you, once you travelled?" he asked, his scales shimmering in the sunlight coming in from the window. "They taught you how to manage your magic, and your emotions?"

I nodded, "Especially when I could pay for the knowledge." I fiddled with my hair, tying it up into a high ponytail. Hints of my natural colour were returning, after years of my dying it each time I changed my name. I didn't mind that the beginnings of grey now peppered its deep auburn tones. My hazel eyes glistened as I calmed, comfortable with myself – finally.

I sat on the edge of the sofa, still with the envelope in my hand. Did I want to know which of my old clients had begun searching for, and more disturbingly, found, Freida? No...Yes...

Coffee.

Before my brain exploded, or I discovered who'd found me and if they posed a threat to my current life, I needed caffeine. I threw the envelope onto the kitchen bench, smiling as Mystara sidestepped, har-rumphed and flew over to the windowsill.

As I boiled the kettle, the possibilities of the unopened letter played on my mind. The familiar whoosh of air as my energy caused a mini whirl wind in my apartment, reminding me why I didn't bother decorating. I stirred my coffee with intention, releasing fear and anxiety.

"You know that caffeine causes agitation?" my dragon asked, "Would wine be a better option?"

"No! I haven't touched a drop of alcohol for years. Wine amplifies my moods, causing more magic to escape. It would be a ginormous backward step to start sipping that poison again." Alcohol, more than caffeine, sparked my agitation, my fear, and other emotions I worked hard at letting go. Magic – I still wasn't sure if that was the name for the energy that ran deep in my veins. Wasn't magic supposed to be a positive thing? My powers had caused me nothing but grief.

I side-eyed the letter, pretending to ignore it, as I drank my coffee. I tended to have an overactive imagination – this letter was probably harmless. Whatever the sender wanted to tell me, could wait. The week between Christmas and New Year was hectic, with last minute sales – indie authors were keen to plug their books. Thankfully, with the internet, I could do my job without leaving my apartment. Even my mail was delivered to my door.

A flash of light told me Mystara had grown sick of my indecision. He often disappeared, and when I asked why, I never received a satisfactory answer. It didn't worry me, having a pint-sized magical creature in my life was by far the coolest thing.

I scrolled through the list of tasks on my to do list. My agoraphobia seemed to be improving. I could walk outside, around the corner to the coffee cart for a real coffee. I'd even made it to the corner shop for groceries, though it was easier to plan ahead and order groceries to be delivered to my door. Something I could never figure out – why could I travel around the world, plane hop, take buses, see all the sights of the world, yet leaving my apartment in the middle of Sydney, felt insurmountable? Returning to my old hometown – home city – had been accidental. On a planned trip from Edinburgh to Melbourne, I'd stopped briefly in Sydney, found a job and an apartment and never made it to the city further south.

"Once I finished the marketing for *Marie Bright and the Toymaker*, then I'll venture further outside – Melbourne – or maybe back to Edinburgh." I talked to myself quite often. Since I lost my old confidante Midnight the black cat who followed me home, years ago in London, each apartment I lived in felt so empty. Talking aloud helped me feel in control. I tasted blood, and realised I'd bitten my lip, as I thought about getting a new pet.

My mobile beeped, startling me. My coffee mug clattered on the marble kitchen bench top. I rarely received calls or messages, unless it was work. The message was cryptic –

Need your help...find the missing book...by the end of the year...

I didn't recognise the number, and had no idea who'd be asking me to find a book? It could be a message about one of the books I was due to finish editing or developing a social media package for. That would be more likely than someone who knew me as Freida, Martha, or even Eliza having followed me halfway around the world.

I eyed the envelope suspiciously. If I wrote mystery stories myself, this would be a perfect way to start. It certainly piqued my curiosity. I held the envelope up to the light, hoping for a clue. I knew why I hesitated – opening this could – or would drag me back into that world of mystery, intrigue, and danger. I needed a distraction.

Stepping outside my apartment was easier than I'd imagined. Leaving my mobile inside had been a stroke of genius. I followed the smell of coffee beans. It wasn't a long walk. The coffee van set up a couple of doors down from the entrance to my apartment block. The worn shopfront behind it, boarded up with cardboard and newspapers, was faded from years of morning sun shining on it. The van, by contrast dressed in orange, lime green and yellow. Fresh, bright, eye catching, and popular.

I stood quietly in line, the voice in my head screaming at my body to be still. The last thing I wanted was for the pent-up energy to escape and create havoc. I tapped my right foot, ever so slightly, releasing a wave of energy out into the ground. Each small ripple on such a busy street, no one would notice. If I stamped my foot, like that time when I was at high school...I shuddered on the inside at the memory.

"The longest day ever," The blonde in line in front of me spoke to her friend, an older woman with grey hair. They were dressed in similar black pant suits. Probably from one of the offices across the road. The accountants, or maybe the solicitors.

"Thank goodness for afternoon coffee breaks," the older woman agreed. "I thought that meeting was going to go on forever."

After a few minutes it was my turn to order. "I'll have an espresso, no, a mocha." I tried to sound decisive, like I regularly ordered coffee and knew what I wanted.

The cute barista smiled and begun to create my order. "I haven't seen you here for a while, have you been away for work?" I didn't like sharing my business with anyone, but I knew he was making small talk.

"I work from home; I tend to stay inside a lot." I shrugged. "I felt like stretching my legs, and a coffee. But there are so many flavours, I couldn't decide what to order." I grinned.

Shortish sandy coloured hair, blue eyes that sparkled when he smiled, I guessed we were similar in age, and I'd be forty in a couple of years. "I'm honoured that you chose my humble establishment. I hope to see you again soon." The barista grinned as he handed me my take-away mug. I knew he was just making small talk, as he did with all his customers, but still, I felt lighter. What I called my energy, buzzed around my body. I'd forgotten the adrenaline rush that went along with human contact. As high as my energy soared, it came crashing back to earth with a thud as I remembered what happened when I let my emotions get the better of me. With a little wave, I hurried back to my apartment, sipping the heavenly drink as I did so.

Chapter Two

The pinging of my mobile distracted me. Reading manuscripts for a small publishing company was another of the hats I wore. I'd started reading at 7am, during the first cuppa of the morning. My mobile had started ringing and sending me the same cryptic message, as the day before, around the same time. Four hours later the buzzing of the phone was relentless. Half a dozen beeps later, was enough to drive me to distraction. I rubbed my temples, where a migraine was hiding, gently throbbing, waiting to take hold. I threw my mobile to the couch, where it proceeded to ping and beep. I didn't bother looking at the caller identification. Chances are it'd be the same number that sent the cryptic message yesterday, and that started ringing, every few hours since then. I clenched and unclenched my fists, a trick I used to steady my emotions – impatience, anxiety, anger, frustration.

The red light on the television indicating it was on standby, flickered off. The digital clock on the microwave blinked off. I tried the kettle and confirmed the power outage. This was the reason I rarely watched television or listened to the radio. My energy, when riled up, tended to mess with the electromagnetic fields of electrical devices. I found it better not to turn them on than to have to replace broken appliances. Luckily this happened less and less these days. Until I received the letter, and the telephone messages.

"Why couldn't it be a long lost relative, or a friend, just ringing to say hi, Merry Christmas and Happy New Year?" I muttered aloud. Not that I often yearned for a normal life with family and friends. Past experiences had proven too painful to continue to on a path that led to pain. Growing up was just me and my parents, and we'd not been close. *For goodness sake Jane, get over yourself.* I stood, stretching my arms, then my legs. There were advantages to being a free spirit, unencumbered. I didn't have to answer to anyone. Except work deadlines.

The manuscript in front of me, a murder mystery, where the main character was a witch, who returned to her hometown and ended up smack bang in the middle of a murder, took advantage of the popularity of the genre. Well written, with all the quirks and whimsy of the paranormal world. Set in a small country town during Halloween, where magic ran through the place, breathing life into all sorts of mythical creatures.

I'd lost concentration, with my mobile beeping, and thinking about my past, the life I could have had, if I'd not possessed magic. Would I've been happy as a housewife, instead of my gypsy life where I was blessed to see so much of our world? I loved my life traveling and living in many exotic places. My fiancé did me a favour, breaking off our engagement, citing I'd changed. He wasn't comfortable with my weird powers. Back then I didn't know why it stormed when I was upset, or why electrical appliances stopped working around me. Items falling off shelves when I walked through a room, and other strange occurrences made life a little tricky. Throughout my travels I learnt a little about magic and people who were able to manipulate the elements. I moved enough that my unusual skills didn't cause any concern. Eventually I learnt tricks to tame my emotions and behaviour. Leaving my phone where it sat, I left my apartment for the second time in two days.

I'd forgotten how hot and humid Sydney could be at the end of December. I nearly ducked back inside for a lighter shirt, but I knew I'd probably not venture back out. Instead, I shrugged my shirt, moving air around, and pushed up the long sleeves on my loose-fitting crème shirt.

The cute barista smiled. "I knew you'd be back. Couldn't resist my coffee." He winked. "Same as yesterday?" He picked up a large plastic cup and started the coffee process.

"Thanks, but I'd like to try something else." The barista, whose name was Dane, according to the name embroidered on his shirt, was a little taller than me, with sandy hair, slightly wavy, not too long. On appearances only, he was nothing like the type I usually found myself involved with. Dark haired, broody men who fell in lust with my wavy red hair, my green eyes, and my stubbornness.

"How about a double shot caramel latte?" Dane began the coffee before I had a chance to answer the question.

"Sounds perfect," I finally managed to squeak out, feeling the familiar heat in my cheeks. Hopefully Dane was too busy making coffee to notice. I'd expected the cart to be swarming with customers, but I wasn't complaining that I had the handsome barista to myself.

Our hands touched as he handed me a large to-go cup. "Let me know if you like it," I knew Dane meant the caramel latte, but I enjoyed the sensation of the brief touch.

"Thanks Dane," I returned his smile. The urge to head back to the sanctuary of my apartment, clashed with the warm fuzzy feeling in my chest, at sharing a smile with a handsome barista. I'd completed my deadline, and had no specific reason to return, but I could hardly stand and chat to Dane. Customers had begun lining up for their pre-lunch time cups of coffee.

Strangely, I didn't feel like returning to my apartment. I stepped to one side as Dane served the woman behind me. Dressed in a suit, like a few of the others milling around the coffee cart, she worked at one of the dozen or so businesses that bordered the busy street. I headed for the only green space within a reasonable walking distance.

The park wasn't large. Half a city block, cleverly designed, incorporated a children's play area in the middle of native bushes and shrubs, around which stood taller, older native trees. Magpies warbled to each

other, wrens and smaller birds flew in around the bushes and a kook-
aburra laughed.

I sat on one of the benches dotted along the path. I liked my life,
enjoyed my own company, my independence and my job. Did I want
the complication of a relationship?

The hairs on the back of my head prickled, as I sensed eyes watching
me. Paranoid? Maybe. It'd been a few years since my private investigator days. I'd not thought of that part of my life since returning to Sydney and starting my other business. If an envelope for Freida hadn't arrived, I'd probably still be focused solely on editing and social media.

Could I be in any danger? Not likely, but I couldn't rule it out.
Whoever wrote to Freida at my address knew where I lived. I really
should open that letter, to put my mind at ease, or worse case, so I knew
what I was up against.

I sighed and headed back towards my apartment. I needed to read
that letter, to figure out what was going on. I grabbed the couple of envelopes that waited for me on the table beside my front door.

My mobile pinged as I opened my door. I cringed. A took a breath
and scrolled through my missed calls and messages. The latest notification was an email indicating I had another manuscript to edit. The other messages mirrored yesterdays –

Need your help...find the missing book...by the end of the year...

The end of the year was only a couple of days away.

Chapter Three

I looked at the pile of mail I'd picked up on my way inside. The security guards delivered mail that arrived for long-time residents. Without flicking through the envelopes, I tossed the whole lot onto the lounge. I'd look at them later, after I read the manuscript – *Edward the Awkward Emu*. A children's book about neurodivergent children and their emotions. The process took longer than I thought. Sometimes editing children's books took longer than a fifty-thousand-word manuscript.

I stretched, rising to look out the window, where the reddish hues of the evening sky quickly danced across the horizon, in between the tall buildings. The city lights prevented the darkness of the night sky to fully descend.

The gurgling in my stomach reminded me I'd skipped lunch, too engrossed in how to best portray an awkward emu. I placed my hands over my tummy. "Time for food." I told the empty apartment. Opening my fridge revealed a few pieces of fruit, some chocolate, and half a carton of milk. Five minutes later I'd fashioned a feast – strawberries, slices of apple, kiwifruit, chocolate, coffee and adding some crackers I discovered lurking in my pantry.

I had a knack of putting off uncomfortable tasks, like returning phone calls, or opening mail. Contact with people, even reading mail, made my head hurt, and my heart ache. It wasn't my fault that my fiancé dumped me, or that my parents died of unrelated illnesses, within a few months of each other a couple of years ago.

Being informed about these events via mail fed my fear of opening letters. My fiancé's note was accusatory – squarely placing the blame on me. The solicitor's correspondences regard each of my parents' deaths implied I should have known of my parents health and been involved in their care. Which would have been true if my parents had told me of any issues when I rang them each week. I sighed. I couldn't put it off any longer.

A few pamphlets advertising local eateries went straight into the bin. I didn't mind takeaways, but as a creature of habit, I'd make my own choice on where to eat, and when. A couple of obligatory Christmas cards from authors and companies I'd worked with throughout the year. The letter addressed to my alter ego taunted me. With all the other mail open, I reached for the mysterious envelope.

I couldn't have guessed the contents of the crisply folded paper, typed neatly with an old-fashioned machine. I ran my fingers over the slight indents the typewriter keys made on the parchment. Brett Bently, an eccentric millionaire employed me over ten years ago, as Freida, to discover who'd been embezzling from his international electronics company. It'd been easier than I'd expected, to figure out it was his wife who'd engineered the fraud. I'd been paid handsomely for my time and effort. In the intriguing letter, Brett Bently dangled a mystery, more fascinating than those I reviewed for aspiring authors.

Freida, I need your help. As my company grows even bigger, creating leading edge apps, hardware, and software, I've had death threats, and long-lost relatives claiming rights to my money and my name. There's a family heirloom – a book – that's gone missing. Someone is threatening to destroy the book, which will destroy me. B.

I recognised the eccentric writing of the millionaire, who I'd developed a soft spot for, when I'd worked for him. His wife had done her best to ruin him personally and professionally. I re-read the note, turning it over, to make sure I didn't miss any details. There were no other clues on the envelope. I remembered the text message, about a book –

Brett must have found my mobile number as well. With his resources and knowledge of technology it wouldn't be difficult for him to find my address and mobile number.

Before I could talk myself out of it, I dialled the number. Brett answered on the first ring. "Freida, or should I call you Jane now? I hope you're calling because you'll agree to help me, before it's too late."

I couldn't help grinning as I remembered Brett's flair for the dramatic. A millionaire who became a billionaire – he worked tirelessly for every single penny. Blonde curly hair, piercing blue eyes, and a faultless smile, we clicked, as friends, "Brett! Apologies for the delay in responding, I've been busy. I hear you have a mystery you need help with."

"Freida, er, Jane, if you could see your way to helping me, in between assignments, I'd be ever so grateful. The book is a family heirloom; someone stole it right out of the glass case where it was on display in my offices. I should never have listened to my marketing person, who insisted it would be safe there. I can send you photos." His normally calm and confident voice sounded dishevelled...if I didn't know better, I'd have said Brett Bently sounded scared.

"Please send me photos and any information you think may be useful. Your text mentioned needing it found by the end of the year, which is only a couple of days away. Why the tight timeframe?"

"I was being melodramatic, hoping to entice you into assisting me," the inflection in his voice told me Brett was lying, but I couldn't figure out why. One mystery at a time.

"Do you have any idea who could have stolen it or why?" I started making notes on the back of the envelope.

"I have a few suspicions. I'll send you an email, and thank you. I've got to run, but we'll talk soon." Brett ended the call, leaving me wondering why he'd just not emailed me in the first place, rather than leaving cryptic messages on my phone and going to the trouble of delivering a note to my home. Unless I'd set all the emails from my clients from my past careers to go to spam.

A check of my computer revealed I'd done just that. With a few clicks on my keyboard, I fixed the situation and settled into read Brett's emails.

I was surprised to read that Brett and his personal assistant Kathy were currently in Sydney at a conference. I'd met Kathy when I'd worked with her boss. It didn't surprise me they were still together ten years later. She was blonde, petite, with a brilliant mind and a terrific personality.

His emails omitted to reveal several important snippets of information. Why did the book need to be found by the end of the year? Why would he lie about it? The Bently family heirloom looked to be about half the size of an A4 piece of paper and as thick as a packet of matches. It's green velvet cover appeared to be in good condition, noting the age of the tome. I recognised the triquetra on the front – the power of three – used by pagans as a powerful protection and good luck symbol.

Brett wasn't very forthcoming, about the contents of the book or why anyone would want to steal it. "I mean, I know it's old, maybe worth money because of who it belonged to." I told my empty apartment. I could think of a few people who'd want to take the object, to annoy him, and make him appear weak. Starting with his wife, competitors in the tech business, and who knows how many others.

Although it was getting late, I wasn't tired. I read as much information as I could find on the internet about Brett, his family, their fortune, and their heirlooms. His corporation relied on innovative ways to utilise state of the art technology. The irony that the family heirloom wasn't safe in the office of a tech giant wasn't lost on me.

One of Brett's emails mentioned a couple of members of staff. He didn't accuse them of anything, but I read between the lines. I looked up them up online. Stanley Con, Gerard Meere and Cody Lee. All intelligent businessmen, gifted in the field of technology, and all currently in Sydney until the end of the year, attending the same conference that lured Brett and Kathy to Australia.

I'd agreed to join Brett for breakfast at his hotel at 7am the next morning. I wasn't looking forward to the short bus ride there, but I knew the trip well enough, having stayed at the same hotel when I'd first arrived in Sydney. After checking the bus company site five times, to confirm I could catch a bus at 6:30am that would definitely take me to where I needed to be, I set my alarm for 5am and finally hopped into bed. My brain was whirring, the migraine had eased off, but the buzz of a new mystery always energised me. I tried reading one of the manuscripts on my reading list, but the words jumbled together. In the end I fell asleep watching reruns of an old British murder mystery on my laptop.

The first light peeped through my curtains before my alarm woke me. I'd been clock watching since before the clock ticked over to 4am. I gave in, my feeble attempt at grabbing just a few more minutes snooze wasn't fooling anyone.

I hardly ever took my laptop out of the apartment now that I worked from home. Rummaging in my wardrobe I recovered the brown leather bag that used to carry my laptop to other jobs. Black jeans, a pink shirt and my black boots, my hair tied back into a ponytail, and I even had time for a cuppa as I added my pen and notepad to my bag. "Keys, wallet, phone..." What else would I need?

6am. Still too early for the bus, but I couldn't sit still any longer. Heaving my backpack onto my shoulder, I locked my door and headed out. The strong aroma of coffee hit me as soon as I opened the door to the street. Even at this early hour, the coffee van was deep in customers. I couldn't stop the smile that played on my lips. The bus stop was only a few metres from the van; there was plenty of time to caffeinate.

"Three days in a row, and so early in the morning!" Dane smiled. He was wearing a deep blue shirt which accentuated his eyes. "Did you run out of coffee, or milk?" He teased.

I returned his smile. "I'd no idea you opened this early. I have an early meeting. I came down to catch the bus, catching a coffee as well is an awesome bonus."

Dane's smile grew wider. "I'm pleased to hear you are happy to see me, or at least my coffee. What'll it be today? Espresso, latte, mocha?"

"Hmm, surprise me. I'd be happy with any option you choose." The butterflies in my stomach had nothing to do with hunger pains, though I did need to remember to buy food at some point during the day. Dane greeted a couple of early morning men in suits as they approached the van. I stepped to one side as he took their order.

A few minutes later he handed me a large mug. "I hope you like it. And I hope to see you when you return from your meeting." I knew Dane probably flirted with all his clients, but still, I couldn't wipe the smile off my face, as I waited for the bus.

"Does this bus go to the Koala Hotel?" I asked the bus driver as I boarded the bus.

"It does." He nodded to the ticket machine, which looked far more complicated than it needed to be. I noted the absence of a space to insert coins or paper money. Not a fan of using my debit card, I nonetheless tapped my card against the blue grey metal machine. The contraption spat out a ticket which could have taken me all the way to the airport, had that been where I wanted to go. I quickly shuffled into a seat close to the front. The grey fake leather seat wasn't damaged so much a scratched, as if a small child or a cat had been picking at the seams.

I'd barely had time to count the stitching, the seats or my fellow passengers, before it was time to alight from my transport. Walking the few metres to the front of the hotel I was going to be early for my breakfast date. People swarmed past. I counted at least twenty on foot, scooters and bicycles in the short space between the bus stop and the driveway for the hotel. Twice as many vehicles – mostly cars, a couple of trucks a bus or two and motorbikes travelled noisily along the road on their way to their destination. I hated crowds. A more accurate assessment would be that I intensely disliked being in a crowd, because I picked up on the emotions and energy of everyone around me. For some reason here in Australia it was more acute then elsewhere.

My studies indicated I wasn't crazy. The gift of being an empath, with the ability to tune into the health and or emotions of others, was another of my crosses to bear. I still had panic attacks if I found myself surrounded, but I could talk myself down before it got out of hand.

I focused my brain on Brett and solving the mystery. I concentrated on walking, one foot after the other. Slow, steady, softly – along the path up to and inside the hotel to the restaurant where the continental breakfast was being served. A stray bolt of energy escaped through my foot. No one noticed, with the rumble of the trucks passing by. Another stray bolt, out through my clenched fist, at the same time as a jack hammer started in a neighbouring alley.

A deep breath in, hold for three and release. I entered through the sliding doors as I exhaled. The bright lights matched the bright smiles of the staff. I returned the smile of the young lass on reception as I turned towards the restaurant. "I'm meeting someone for breakfast." I smiled sweetly at the other, nearly identical, smartly dressed brunette who stood at the dais in the entry to where the tables were set for breakfast.

"Room number?" she asked, with a smile.

"Probably the penthouse," I said, knowing Brett.

"You must mean Mr Bently," she said knowingly. "Take a seat at table thriteen. He rang ahead and said he will be here by 7am."

As I thanked her and headed to the table, a familiar voice boomed behind me, "Freida! Early as usual."

I couldn't help smiling, despite the fact Brett used my old name. I turned, "Brett, Kathy, so nice to see you both again." We shook hands. Customers eating their breakfast hardly gave us a second look. Dressed in business suits, noses in their tablets, laptops or mobiles, busy catching up on news or work before heading into their offices, conferences or whatever they had to be. Table thirteen sat at the back of the eating area.

The table was set for three, although six could easily have fitted with plenty of elbow room. I'd noticed the buffet set up, and people serving themselves. Not normally a breakfast person, I'd been considering what foods I might choose. I didn't need to worry about that, as within seconds of sitting down a smartly dressed waiter with a tray arrived at our table.

"I hope you don't mind Freida, but I took the liberty of ordering breakfast for the three of us. A selection of all that's on offer, coffee and juice as well, to be delivered to the table. We need to talk, and we don't have time to waste choosing out own food." So very Brett, I thought, as the waiter handed out plates of hot food to each of us. A platter of pastries and fruit sat in the middle, the bigger table made sense now, along with a pitcher of juice and a second filled with coffee.

It felt like we'd last seen each other last week, not nearly ten years ago. "Very thoughtful, considered, and sensible." I agreed. "Can you try to remember to call me Jane? I haven't been Freida for such a long time."

Kathy's head bobbed up and down. "I did try to remind him," she said apologetically, "But you may remember Brett, when he gets something in his head..."

"Stubborn, you mean," I quipped.

"Takes one to know one," was his smart return.

I held my hands up in mock surrender. "Okay, okay, Freida it is then, I suppose I don't mind, and it'll help switch my mindset from editor and social media back to private investigator."

"Great. Now that's settled, what questions do you have for me?" Brett wasted no time, digging into his plate piled high with sausage, bacon, egg, tomato, mushroom, baked beans and toast. I looked at my plate with an identical full English breakfast, and realised I was starving. I rarely ate meat anymore, but not because I was opposed to it, I just didn't like cooking. I watched Kathy and Brett eat as I considered his question.

"I read a lot online, about you, what you've been up to in the last ten years. I read about your family artefacts, why you are here in Sydney, and about the three people you mentioned. What I want to know is, what wouldn't I have read, that is important? What else do I need to know, to solve this problem. For example, is there a time imperative, and if so, why?"

Chapter Four

Rather than stare at Brett, waiting for answers, I started on my hot breakfast. The taste of food I'd not eaten in years, was a pleasant explosion on my taste buds. The texture of the meats and eggs nearly made me gag, because I'd not prepared myself for it. Thankfully I'd deliberately cut small portions as I chose to swallow quickly and wash the mouthful down with juice. If either of my table mates noticed they respectfully refrained from commenting.

"Right to the point as usual. Which is why I need you to solve this. Asap." Brett nodded thoughtfully. "Stanley, Gerard and Cody have all separately challenged my leadership. They don't have claims on the business, but they own shares in companies set up under the umbrella of Bently Enterprises. Those loyal to me have advised there is a takeover planned for New Year's Day." He paused and sipped his coffee. I waited impatiently for him to continue. "If they pool their shares together, while they won't have a majority, they will be in a strong position." Another pause, another sip of coffee. I bided my time, returning his gaze. I remembered this dance. "That little book of my mother's, her great great grandmothers initially, is said to contain magic, protection, and all my good fortune. All I know is that I've always been prosperous, stupidly lucky with everything I've tried. Until now. Since the book disappeared I've lost clients. Big clients that our company couldn't afford to lose. Our stock prices have plummeted. We can't buy the metals and raw materials we need. It's as if someone has cursed us. Which is ridiculous and I don't believe in all that woo woo stuff," He added quickly.

I looked from Brett to Kathy, processing what I'd just heard. I'd not taken notes but had no doubt I'd remember all the main points. I did believe in *woo woo* as Brett worded it, but I wasn't sure it was the cause in this case.

Kathy lay her knife and fork gently on her plate. "Those three are definitely looking to ruin Brett," her voice was quiet but there was a force behind it. "Over the last six months they've each tried to date me, which was weird, but I shut each one down." She side-eyed Brett, "I didn't tell you because I knew you'd be furious."

"Are you two officially an item yet?" I asked gently.

The couple exchanged a glance so intense that I turned away. "No, yes – we spend every waking hour together," was Brett's response.

"Okay, so whose idea was it to move the book from the mansion to the display case at the office?" I knew the office and the mansion were equipped with state-of-the-art security measures. Clearly something had failed. It would be a sore point for my friend who was used to controlling everything. No wonder we got on so well.

"Mine." Kathy's eyes filled with tears. "I overheard some clients speaking about how amazing Brett was and how they'd like to know more about him as a person, what made him the billionaire he is today. I thought bringing in some family relics might make clients and staff relate to him more easily." I had to look away, the remorse on her face too raw.

"I've been called aloof, unapproachable," he shrugged. "I don't blame Kathy, she thought she was helping." Brett controlled his voice. The veins in his neck betraying the tension in his body. The fists clenched his cutlery, as he held himself so tightly wound up, close to breaking.

"Unclench your hands and let go the cutlery before the knife flies around and injures someone," I said sternly.

My words broke the tension at the table. Kathy laughed nervously as Brett placed his knife and fork on the edge of his plate.

"Your security system – you would've checked the footage around the time the book went missing. You probably updated security measures, fired the security team, and got a new contractor on board. Have you searched the employees? What else have you done to resolve the issue, and how are your employees holding up?" My heart pounded as I rattled off the items I'd have checked straight after the theft.

Brett looked fondly at me. "See Kathy, this is why we have Freida, er Jane on board. Our security system experienced a glitch that lasted for three hours around the time the book was stolen. Unrecoverable footage. I kept the company on, because I'm holding them to account and they've promised to fix it by whatever means possible, or I don't pay them anything. It surprised me when they agreed to that. All employees were searched, their work areas, lockers etc. My legal team wouldn't agree to me searching their cars or homes. Most employees are on Christmas holiday leave. Before you ask, we, and those three I mentioned before are at this conference. The event is held annually, but at different locations around the globe. It's called a conference, but it's more of a way to wind down after a busy year, looking at how *technology can be used for recreation* showcase."

"Is the event here, at this hotel?" I remembered the renovations and building work that occurred during my stay here.

"Yes, the whole event takes place here. We don't have to leave, apart from catching the shuttle to the airport when it's time to return to the UK," Kathy gushed. The colour had returned to her cheeks; she was her normal bubbly self.

"Can I meet them? Cody, Stanley, and Gerard?" I asked, proud of myself for remembering their names without referring to my notepad or laptop.

"I'm not sure that would work, they don't know that I'm talking to you or that I consider them a threat. At least I don't think they do," Brett picked up a pastry covered in hazelnut spread and chocolate chips. I followed his lead, as did Kathy.

Before popping a piece of the pastry into her mouth she nodded at table nine, across from us. "Gerard has the grey beard, Cody the short dark cropped hair and Stanley's bald with glasses." All three had their noses in their laptops, coffee in one hand, and an eclair in the other.

I ignored the frown Brett gave his personal assistant. "Brett, I'm offended, did you think I'd jump up and introduce myself to your colleagues?" I pretended to be hurt, although it was exactly what I wanted to do, and he knew it. I once confronted his wife in front of a room of socialites, about her infidelities and fraud. "I won't," I added gently, "I can see you are upset about this. If they don't know you suspect them, and are planning a takeover, I don't want to tip their hand."

The relief in his face was palpable. "I suppose I could introduce you as an old friend I ran into while we were in Sydney," he suggested. "If they ask or come over to say hello."

That was fair, but before I could comment, Brett's phone rang, belting out the tune of an old eighties song he liked. "Excuse me, I'd better get this," he dragged his chair back, and headed for a quiet corner by the window. Whilst he was gone, I studied the table of three men who potentially posed a threat to my friend's company.

"Do you like Sydney, and your new career choice?" Kathy piped up, either to fill in the silence or because she was genuinely interested. "I've always lived in the same city, and I've worked for Brett since I left university. You're so brave. I admire your ability to re-invent yourself."

"Consider yourself lucky you haven't had to re-invent yourself," I replied. "It's a lot of hard work, remembering the changes you have to make to your life. Leaving behind people who matter, if you have people who matter, and I think you do." I glanced at Brett.

Kathy blushed. "I don't want to go anywhere, at least not without Brett," she whispered. "With him I get to see parts of the world I'd never visit by myself, and he's good to me, it's just..."

"You want your relationship to progress to the next level, and he likes it just the way it is," I finished her sentence for her.

Her face got even redder. "You are good at this."

"Thank you. It's a knack I have – reading people. It can be useful, but it can also get me into trouble."

Brett arrived back at the table before we could finish our discussion. His face was pale, drawn. As he plonked himself on the chair, it wobbled, I leant my hand on it to steady it.

Kathy reached over, patting Brett's arm. "What's wrong?"

"My home was broken into. Which shouldn't be possible." His voice shook with a rage I recognised from my initial investigations for him. Finding out his wife had been cheating on him and embezzling from his company just about killed him. "I've just fired the security company, which in hindsight probably wasn't the best idea. Apparently, my office and most other rooms were ransacked. Thank goodness I'd given the staff the week off. I wouldn't know what to do if any of them had been injured."

"Mr and Mrs Kenny must be in their eighties now, are they still chief housekeeper and groundsman?" I understood Brett's concern. I'd developed a soft spot for them. Kind and helpful, they wouldn't speak a word against Brett or his wife.

"Late seventies, and yes, though they have staff to delegate to. They're still in charge there." His bottom lip trembled. "They came home to the mess after a couple of days with their families. After the police are finished, they'll be coordinating the clean-up." He pushed his plate into the middle of the table. Picking up his empty cup he gazed into it, before returning it to its saucer.

"Why don't we go home and help them?" Kathy suggested. "You don't need to be here. Your keynote was yesterday. If you need any messages delivered, as much as you distrust them, I am sure they can pass on the information." She gestured to the occupants of table nine.

"I agree with Kathy. If they're innocent, they'll want to help. If they're part of a plot against you, they'll be happy you are leaving, but will want to make sure the company survives." An idea came to me. "Introduce me as an old family friend. Give them my number in case there's any information they need to pass on and they can't get hold of you. Who knows, they might let something slip." Kathy and Brett looked done in. They wanted to be stoic, but I knew they were concerned about leaving the clean up to the Kennys'. "If you can get a last-minute flight out and leave asap, it'll put your mind at rest."

Kathy pulled out her mobile, punching in a number before I finished speaking. "Any chance of two tickets on a direct flight to London? Now. One stopover – the least number of hours possible. Right, Twelve? She looked at her watch. We can manage that. Thank you." She laid her phone on the table. "Brett, introduce Freida to the boys. I'll go and pack our stuff and ring a taxi. We've got two hours to get to the airport and another two hours to get through customs." Her mobile pinged. "The tickets are here, on my phone. Freida, Jane, it was lovely to see you again, even though the circumstances weren't ideal." Her hand briefly touched mine and she was off, through the reception area where I lost sight of her.

"Look after her Brett, she dotes on you. You're very lucky."

"I am," his voice wobbled as his cheeks reddened. "Now, and please don't let me regret this, let me introduce you to the others." He led me to where the tech guys were standing, gathering up their electronics, having finished their breakfast. "Cody, Stanley, Gerard," Brett pointed to each man, "I'd like you to meet Freida. Her family and mine go way back. I've just had some bad news, and I must return home straight away. If you need to reach me but you can't get through, Freida has generously agreed to me passing her contact details on to you. There shouldn't be a problem, but you know how things go, even for a company that specialises in technology." He added wryly. "I'll see you next week, for our weekly meeting. Now Freida, please let me walk you out."

"Nice to meet you," I smiled and shook hands with each of Brett's colleagues. As we left their table, I whispered, "Nice trick, walking me out so that I don't stay behind and grill them about the issues with the company." I felt Brett tense beside me. "I'm joking," I added. A quick sideways glance behind me confirmed they'd left the restaurant.

A couple of steps from the door, I turned and hugged Brett. Impulsively, I didn't make a habit, when I was a private eye, of hugging my clients. "Take care, my friend. Keep Kathy close. Let me know when you're home. Give my love to the Kennys'. I'll send you updates as I have them. We'll talk when you land."

Tears filled my eyes as I walked towards the bus stop. I had a bad feeling about this.

Chapter Five

I knew from my own travels that Brett and Kathy would be cutting it fine, getting to the airport in time for their flights. The trip would involve just over twenty-four hours in the air, depending on the length of the stopover. I hoped Kathy managed to get them premium seats. It made for a slightly better experience.

Being in limbo thousands of metres in the air, while life went on in London, Sydney, and everywhere else was an unusual feeling. Time blurred together and when travelling to the UK, moving backwards in time. I shook my head to clear my thoughts and boarded the bus back to my apartment. Should I return to the hotel to interrogate the suspects? Maybe, but Brett, and Kathy, needed me to be clear headed and focused on reuniting Brett with his family heirloom.

A tall, lanky youth with a backpack slung over his shoulder, and a skateboard under his arm jostled past me. Across the aisle a young man, with ear pods, a leather briefcase and shiny leather shoes, scrolled through his tablet. There was something familiar about him. Probably looked like someone I'd passed by on my way here. The bus was crowded for its return journey, stopping several times to let passengers off and collect new ones. The harried mother with the babe in a carrier slung to her chest with a toddler holding her free hand. An older woman, dressed in a beige shirt and brown shirt, with her tote bag tucked on her shoulder. A group of men and women, dressed in black with coloured shirts.

I ran through the problem in my head. The trip wasn't long enough to start making notes. Brett had three people possibly vying to take over his business. I made a mental note to ask him if there was any proof, beyond office gossip. Apart from the book, was anything else stolen from the office or the mansion? On the chance that Brett or Kathy still had Brett's phone switched on I sent a quick message – *Was anything else stolen, or just the book? Have there been any formal notice of intended takeover / challenge to business? Any idea if anything was stolen at home?*

Not expecting an immediate response, I ran through my options. Was there footage of the break in at the office, or at the mansion? I could contact the Kennys' and ask them myself. Maybe talk informally to Brett's work colleagues. A beep as I left the bus indicated I'd received a response. I stepped to one side, to read the text and let other passengers pass by.

Only book stolen, no formal notice, just heard rumours, murmuring amongst the board, nothing stolen at home, Security footage shows two hooded figures entering through a side door on the verandah and throwing things around. Turning off phone now B x

"Are you lining up for another cuppa?" Dane's voice interrupted my thoughts. Bringing myself back to the present, I smiled at the friendly barista.

"I could be tempted." I noticed the man from the bus was standing to one side, waiting for his order.

"I've a special offer today," Dane continued, as he placed a lid on the mug for the customer waiting by the side of the van. "My sister's a baker and she's made a gazillion macaroons for me to trial with my customers. Would you like one with your coffee?"

Although I'd attempted a big breakfast not so long ago, I loved a sugar hit. "Yes please! Now if you had chairs and tables for customers to sit at while they ate or drank, it'd be perfect." I don't know why I was so chatty all of a sudden.

"I've a little seat behind here if you want to use it." Dane said graciously waving to a portable camping chair behind the van. "Thankfully business is so good that I rarely get to sit down."

"That sounds perfect. My office is such a walk away and I need to sit a while." I glanced at the man from the bus, worried he was following me. Would Dane pick up on my concern and not give away that the building I lived in was less than ten metres away.

With a wink that I don't think anyone else noticed, he offered, "Hop around this side. There's more room behind the van than it looks from the front." He handed me a paper bag with a macaroon and a large cup of mocha, judging by the chocolatey aroma. I placed both on the tiny table in front of me.

"Thanks Dane." I dragged my notepad and pen out of my bag, leaving my laptop where it was. I tucked my bag under the little camp table, where no one could reach it. I sipped my coffee and glanced around the side to where Dane was serving customers.

The man from the bus was standing to one side, doing his best to appear invisible. Head down, reading his phone while sipping from his takeaway cup. His ear pods were firmly in place, maybe he was simply waiting for a work colleague. I did tend to have an overactive imagination which both got me into trouble and was a godsend, depending on the situation.

I pulled the macaroon from its bag. Dane had chosen a soft purple colour for me. It looked amazing, so small it fitted in the palm of my hand. I took a tiny bite. The explosion of sugary sweetness, not too sweet but enough to make me smile. "Your sister should start her own bakery. This is amazeballs." I grinned at Dane.

"Funny you should say that..." he touched his finger to his nose. "I'm sworn to secrecy, but what I can say is...watch this space." As a group of women turned up, chatting about a book they'd been reading for book club, Dane turned back to his customers.

My fellow passenger didn't appear to be moving. What I really wanted to do was go home, spread out my laptop and my notes and solve the mystery. My intuition told me not to reveal to him where I lived. I finished my cuppa and my little piece of sugary heaven. I packed my pen and notepad into my backpack. I tucked the little chair and table together. "Thanks Dane," I wanted to tap him on the shoulder, but I'd only met him a day or two ago. "Have a good day, I might see you again later."

The barista nodded and smiled, busy with the orders of the half a dozen people in front of him. I walked past the man with the ear pods, heading in the opposite direction to my apartment. With a vague idea where I was headed, I moved briskly making it look like I was on my way to work. Office buildings sat alongside shopfronts selling everything from women's clothing to vapes. I discounted the accountants and the stockbrokers. My anxiety hadn't trumped my adrenaline, but a backwards glance told me I was being followed.

Stuff it. I muttered under my breath as I pushed open a door to a solicitor's. The windows and doors of frosted glass prevented my tail from seeing inside. If he didn't follow me inside, I might have lost him.

My thumping heart made it a little difficult to hear the receptionist. I concentrated on reading her lips while I took a couple of calming breaths.

"Hi, yes, I'd like to make an appointment to see a solicitor. To make a will." I didn't need one, with no family or friend to leave my few items to.

The receptionist, a young lady dressed in a pale pink shirt and navy skirt, scrolled her finger down her appointment book. It was refreshing to see old school tools. "I have an opening in half an hour if you'd like to wait." She beamed at me.

"Thank you." I perched on one of the beige armchairs clutching my laptop bag. I couldn't see the street from my position, no matter how I twisted and turned. How long would my tail stay waiting to see if I exited the office? The more I tried not to fidget, the more my legs bobbed up and down. My tricks for calming my anxiety worked, but this was a lot of stress. Sitting in a solicitor's office pretending I needed to make a will, to escape the man following me, I was stronger than that. I should be solving Brett's problem.

I stood, so suddenly that the receptionist looked at me. "Is everything okay?" She asked.

"Yes. I mean, I'm sorry, but I've just remembered that I have another appointment that I can't change. I'll ring you to book another appointment," I replied, with no intention of ever stepping foot inside the building again.

"Sure thing. Here's our card. It has our number, and our email address. Just make contact when you are ready," she gushed, handing me a glossy business card embossed with black and gold.

"Thank you." I tucked the card into the front of my bag, and pulled the door open, crossing my fingers and toes that no one was waiting for me on the other side.

Chapter Six

The street wasn't empty, but I didn't recognise any of the people. If the man had been following me, he wasn't anywhere in sight. I couldn't spot him amongst the crowd of men, women, and children hurrying to and from various destinations. After a quick survey of the area, I headed back toward my apartment. The trip took longer than I remembered, but then I'd been away from my sanctuary for many hours. *You're not doing too badly Jane.* I told myself. *Not long to go now.* I quickened my pace at the thought of another chance to chat to Dane.

"Excuse me dear," a little lady with a shopping cart jostled me. "I'm not as steady on my feet as I used to be. She disappeared into the crowd before I had a chance to reply. I lowered my head, concentrating on the footpath in front of me. In my head I visualised a shield of silver protecting me from the emotions of the people I walked past. My resolve began to waver. Meeting Brett, getting back into my private investigator mode, caught me off guard. The idea that a person had been following me, messed with my head. My anxiety manifested itself, the pounding of my head, the blood thumping through my body.

Slowing my steps, I took longer strides, letting some of my angst flow out and along the footpath. With so many people around, no one would notice the minute vibrations. As I wriggled my toes in my shoes and wiggled my fingers, small bursts of energy released, calming my mood a little. The coffee cart was surrounded by customers. I glanced at my watch, surprised it was only a little after 11am. I caught Dane's eye and smiled, but I kept walking towards my apartment. I needed a few minutes peace, or more likely a few hours, to get my head straight.

I climbed as quickly as my legs let me, up the three flights of stairs to my apartment. I could have taken the lift, but I was a creature of habit. No mail greeted me on the table by my door. *Good, I couldn't have stood any more surprises.*

Rather than another cuppa, I grabbed a bottle of water from my fridge. Sitting at the kitchen bench I took my laptop and notepad from my backpack. I checked my phone, relieved to find no new messages. I didn't expect to hear from Brett or Kathy for at least twenty-four hours.

I browsed the internet for more information on Brett's company and the three men I'd met earlier. Of the three, Stanley stood out as the one most likely to try a hostile takeover. He used to own his own tech company, which was swallowed up by Bently Enterprises during the pandemic. Gerard had taught at university before coming on as one of Brett's head of department. Cody had been described a child genius and used to everyone making a fuss of how intelligent and clever he was. Such a weird mix of bedfellows.

The question – were any of the trio likely to talk to me, or tell me what was going on? Were the three of them even working together? Friends? Work mates? Or conspirators? I needed to speak to them.

I sighed.

I needed a pet. Someone to talk to and run ideas by. My mystical figurine was nowhere to be seen.

I jumped, as my phone vibrated on the bench. I didn't recognise the number. I considered answering but decided whoever it was could leave a message. I tapped my fingers on the bench while I waited to see if a message came in.

I know who you are. We need to meet. Not at the hotel. There's a café – The Coffee Shot. Be there in an hour.

An answer to my questions, or someone who wished me harm? I was pretty sure it was one of the three men I'd met. Which one? Why, what did they want?

Fortunately, I knew of the café he mentioned. It wasn't far from the hotel. My hands shook as I hurriedly returned my laptop to my bag. I made sure my keys, wallet and phone were tucked in the front pocket and raced out the door. When I nearly tripped on the stairs, I forced myself to slow down. If I missed the 12:05 bus, I'd have to wait fifteen minutes for the next one. Memorising things like timetables became a habit on my overseas travel. My anxiety meant I still double and triple checked them.

I only realised I'd been holding my breath as I exhaled, once I exited the building and saw the bus pull in. I'd time only for a quick glance in the direction of the coffee cart. The only empty seat was towards the back of the bus. Not an ideal placement for an agoraphobic. As the bus pulled away from the curb, I allowed myself to speculate.

Who had sent me the text? Were they a supporter of Brett and the company or angling for a position of power? What did *I know who you are* mean? An odd way to initiate contact. Should I have let someone know where I was going? Dane, or one of the security staff at the apartment block. I scoffed at my melodramatic thoughts.

Did Brett introduce me as Jane or Freida? I ran through the morning's introductions in my brain. Jane, I think, yes, I'm positive. I forced my palms open; they were so tightly clenched my nails were starting to leave marks on the flesh. My fingers curled around the metal bar in front of me. Tiny bursts of energy flowed harmlessly from my fingers. I closed my eyes for no more than a nano second. Opening them I glanced furtively at my fellow passengers. No one appeared to be paying me any attention. Noses in books, on their phones, or staring vacantly out the window as the city sped past. Except for the one too skinny, bald guy whose legs were wobbling as he sat hunched over, head in his hands. A threat, no, an addict, maybe. I quickly visualised my protective shield, plugging any gaps in my armour, telling myself how strong, capable and safe I was.

Alighting the bus at the stop nearest the hotel, I loitered to see who else exited. An old woman, a tote bag draped over her arm, muttering to herself as she stepped onto the footpath was the only other passenger to exit. She shuffled along the pavement in the opposite direction. Checking my watch as my feet started walking towards my destination, I'd made it with twenty minutes to spare. I saw the chairs and tables outside *The Coffee Spot,* less than a block away. Forcing myself to breath evenly, I slowed my steps. My fists loosened, letting my energy release harmlessly. As I walked, taking note of my surroundings.

No one appeared to be taking any notice of me or my approach to the popular eatery. All five settings outside were taken, none of the customers were familiar. As I stepped through the doors, a rush of cold air from the air conditioning caused an involuntary shiver down my spine.

I recognised Gerard immediately. Grey beard, glasses on, wearing the same grey suit and shirt he'd been wearing at breakfast. Sitting in one of the corner booths, he sat up straight, staring at the door I'd just entered. I gulped down the lump of bile rising in my throat and headed for the table. I extended my hand. "Good to see you again Gerard." Although I wasn't sure yet if it was in fact good to see him again so soon.

He offered his hand, and we shook. "Freida, thank you for meeting me at such short notice. Apologies for the clandestine nature of the message. Have you heard from Brett?"

"No, and I don't expect to hear from him for at least twenty-four hours. As you'd appreciate that flight is a particularly long one. Unless you travelled here in a less direct route." I ended lamely, realising there were many options for traveling halfway across the world.

Gerard nodded. "I stopped over in a few places, to make the most of the trip. Can I get you anything? Coffee, or a sandwich?"

I was starving, but not keen on sharing a meal with a stranger. "A cup of peppermint tea would be nice, thank you."

Gerard motioned to the waitress with long dark hair tied into a bun. A cup of peppermint tea, and a flat white, with water for the table." He said as she approached the table. She flashed a fake smile and headed back to fulfil our order.

Gerard stared at me, through his thick lensed, square framed glasses. I decided to take the lead. "I must say your message was cryptic. Did you have some information you needed passed on to Brett?" I forced myself to lean back into the hard cushioned seat, hopefully providing the illusion of nonchalance.

"I remember your face. Brett sang your praises back when you helped him with the unfortunate incident of his ex-wife. You were in the office during my first month working there. I must admit to being a little star struck, as an old school university professor, finding myself at Bently Enterprises with the job of engaging the brightest up and coming minds. Little things stuck in my mind. Like the variety of free food and drink in the corporate kitchen area, the comfortable seats, and Brett's tussle with his wife." Gerard hands twisted the paper napkin on the table as he spoke. His actions gave away his nervousness. "I vividly remember Brett pointing to you, as you hopped into the lift after a meeting with him. He said 'Gerard, if you ever have a problem, or a mystery that needs solving, Freida's the person to do it.' I remember being pleased I had no encumbrances, no wives or girlfriends to worry about." He looked at his hands, tried to straighten the napkin, finally tucking it, creased as it was, back under his cutlery.

"So now you have a personal matter that needs to be resolved?" I prompted.

He glanced at me with derision. "Of course not," he retorted, clearly disgusted at the thought. "You misunderstand." He wiggled his back, positioning himself more squarely on his chair. "I recognised you this morning. It occurred to me that Brett may have asked you to investigate the theft of his family heirloom. That being the case, there's something you need to know."

I leant forward a little and waited for him to continue. The waitress placed our cups in front of us. After she returned to the counter, Gerard glanced around the café, as if checking for someone. "Stanley isn't happy with the direction Brett is taking the company. Apparently, Brett promised him more of a leadership role when his company joined with Bently." He picked up his spoon, dragging it around the creamy mix in his cup. I let the gentle aroma of peppermint waft around me. "Brett's more pragmatic. Stanley's company failed, Bently assimilated it, and kept him on as a head of department. Nothing more."

Gerard's information proved my suspicions. "Has Stanley attempted a formal takeover of the company?" Waiting for Gerard to get to the point was like pulling teeth.

"He's trying to garner interest first. He approached me, and the other man you met today, Cody, a childhood genius on all accounts. He's out to further his career but he's not sure who to step on to get there." Gerard held his cup to his mouth, blew on the hot liquid, and tentatively sipped it. "Stanley is threatening to make public some information I'd prefer to stay hidden. So far, I've managed to ignore him. There are others in the company who are willing to join him. The rumour is he'll attempt a takeover on new year's day, UK time."

I sipped my peppermint tea, allowing the fragrance to seep into my senses, both calming and awakening them. "Does Stanley have any weaknesses that you are aware of?"

"I'm trying to stay out of this," he said his voice raising a couple of octaves. "I only mentioned it because I figured Brett has asked you to look into it." He glanced at his timepiece, the gold metal band and clock piece looked heavy, and expensive. "I must go now." He stood and hurried away, without paying for our drinks.

I sighed and drank the rest of my tea. Two drinks wouldn't break my piggy bank.

The waitress looked over my shoulder as I paid our bill. Uninterested, waiting for her shift to be over. I turned and noticed the same man I suspected of following me earlier in the day.

Chapter Seven

It was his leather briefcase and shoes that I recognised at first. Difficult to make out his features as he stood in the shadows, leaning against the wall, just by the door, his face tilted towards the mobile in his hand. I didn't stare too closely, as much as I wanted to. I put my head down and strode through the door as it opened to let a new lot of customers into the restaurant.

I strode purposefully along the path to the bus stop, grateful to find a bus going in the right direction to take me home. I joined the line to board the bus. A couple of teenage girls in sports gear, an older well-dressed gentleman, and a woman with a toddler in her arms, were ahead of me. I swiped my bus pass at the machine where the driver sat, found the closest vacant seat, and slid into it. Behind me a couple of middle-aged women entered, followed by a couple of goths – dressed in black, with pale make up, black lips and eye shadow. They looked all of about twelve.

The man I thought had been following me, did not enter the bus. As I processed this new piece of information, the bus drove away from the curb. Standing back on the edge of the path, the man with the leather case, moved his hand in a half circle in front of his face, giving me a wave.

My anger seethed. He wasn't security, Brett hadn't time to organise that before his flight. The man had the audacity to wave. He knew I knew he was there, and it hadn't fazed him. Did he already know where

I lived, and didn't need to follow me home? How then, did he know I'd be meeting Gerard? No one ever got close enough to me to bug any of my belongings. Did Stanley have a listening devise on Gerard? It seemed the likeliest possibility.

My brain scanned back through the information Gerard had provided. Stanley's takeover would take place in a couple of days, give or take a few hours. Not long after Brett and Kathy landed at Heathrow, unless I could solve the riddle. Who stole the book, where it was, and what significance the book held. Could figuring out the importance of the book unlock the solution? Identifying the thief, returning the book, and preventing the takeover – not a small list of chores for me to achieve in a tight timeframe.

Should I confront Stanley, or speak to Cody? I was so deep in thought, I nearly missed my stop, until I saw the bright colours of Dane's coffee cart.

The area outside the coffee van was crowded. As I got closer, I realised it wasn't just customers, but tradesmen, who were taking up space. The empty shop front behind the van was a flurry of activity. My heart sank into my stomach. If someone opened that shop, would Dane have to move on somewhere else? Having a coffee van in front of a new business wouldn't be conducive to bringing in clients. How far I'd be willing to walk for a coffee, or to see Dane's face, I wasn't sure. A few hundred metres, maybe.

I walked up to the van, where Dane was wiping down the counter top. "If you want a coffee, I could make you an instant, but I've turned off the machines."

"Thanks, but I'm good at the moment." I motioned to the activity behind him. "With the shop opening, I'm guessing you have to move."

"Yes, that's the plan." Dane seemed happier about moving on than I expected. I'd only known him for a couple of days, why did I feel sad that he was moving on?

"Do you know where you are going yet? Will you be far away?" I asked, ignoring the beating of my heart and the heat rising in my cheeks.

The smile on Dane's face grew wider. "Yes." He motioned to the shop front behind him. "My sister and I are setting up shop. She'll be selling her macaroons, her pastries and mini cakes and I'll be expanding on the drinks I make. Coffees, teas, smoothies, milkshakes, maybe juices, eventually."

"Oh Dane, that's a wonderful opportunity for you, and your sister," I added, sounding a little breathless. *What was happening to me, I didn't need a romantic liaison, I needed to solve a puzzle.*

He grinned. "Thanks. Enough about me, I don't even know your name. I mean, mine's emblazoned on my chest, but yours?"

My cheeks flushed. "Jane. Maybe I should get printed shirts?" I returned his grin.

"Forgive me for sounding bold, but you seemed worried, earlier today. Is everything okay?" I sensed genuine concern from the barista.

I tried to smile. "That's so kind of you to ask Dane, seeing as all you know about me is that I don't have a favourite coffee drink." This time my smile felt more genuine. "There's a mystery I need to solve, for a friend of mine, a client really. It's more difficult than it should be. I became a little paranoid, thinking I was being followed."

"I see." Dane stopped cleaning and stared directly at me. "I don't think you were imagining it. That man, with the weird leather shoes walked off in the same direction as you did. I can't guarantee that he was tailing you, but from where I stood, it looked like it." He leant in closer. "Are you in any kind of trouble, danger?"

I decided to answer honestly. "I'm not sure. I could use a sounding board." I indicated the noise going on in the shop behind him. "But I know you are busy with the move. Thanks anyway." I stepped back from the cart, to give Dane an opportunity to continue his cleaning.

Instead, Dane walked around to the front of the cart. "If you are happy to meet Carrie, my sister, and give us a hand with setting up the shop, I'm happy to be your sounding board."

My heart did somersaults. Could he hear the noise it was making, as it pounded in my chest? I nodded, struggling to find my voice. As I trailed behind the barista, I found managed to squeak out, "I'd love to meet your sister, and to help with the café."

Carrie, her long blonde hair tied in a high ponytail, was mopping the powdery blue tiled floor with a sponge mop. Three of the walls were freshly painted a crisp white, the fourth a blue that matched the floor. Dark wooden tables, and bench seat chairs – I counted ten tables and matching chairs, stacked on the wall furthest from the front door. The front counter painted navy, with metal embellishments, and a large display cabinet.

"Sis, I'd like you to meet Jane," Dane led me to his sister.

"Nice to meet you," I held my hand out awkwardly to Carrie, unsure of protocol when meeting people informally.

Fortunately, neither Carrie or Dane batted an eyelid. Carrie shook my hand. "It's nice to meet you too."

"Your macaroons are amazing," I added.

"Thank you." Carrie smiled. "I absolutely love making cute little sweet treats. I'm sure I have some for you to taste test, once I've set up the space. Dane, are you able to help move the furniture into place, once the floor is dry?"

"I'll help," I piped up as Dane nodded his agreement.

"Would you like to tell me the puzzle?" Dane asked as we lifted one of the tables and manoeuvred it into position.

"A client has had a book stolen, from his place of work. The book is a family heirloom. In a maybe unrelated event, one of his board members is planning a hostile takeover. Also, his mansion was broken into, though I've no confirmation of a theft associated with that incident."

I paused as we moved the second table in position. "As I say it all out loud it sounds a little crazy."

Dane looked thoughtful. "Has your client spoken to the police?"

"I'm not sure, but he's not a fan of the way they work. I used to work as a private investigator, and I solved a mystery for him years ago. When the heirloom was stolen, he asked for my help." There was something niggling at the back of my mind, something Brett had told me years ago. It sat on the edge of my consciousness, taunting me.

We moved the rest of the tables in silence. I wasn't sure what to say next. The chairs were heavier than they looked. I hefted one up sideways but rejigged it until I carried it front on.

"Deceptively heavy, aren't they?" Dane chuckled. "I'm not sure whether they'll be too heavy for the customers. We have lighter chairs on order, due to arrive within a week." He lifted the next chair and placed it at one of the tables. "Do you have any suspects? For the theft?"

"A couple of people who work in the company. One of them is trying to takeover, as I mentioned. That's all the information I have. That, and the heirloom is the family's lucky charm, though I'm not certain that's relevant." I wrangled the last chair into place.

Carrie placed a plate of mini pastries on the table we'd just set up. "Some treats to sample." She smiled. "For your hard work so far." Not much bigger than the macaroons and with hazelnut icing and sprinkles the pastries looked amazing. I took a bite, and the sugary, nutty taste exploded, and melted in my mouth simultaneously. "Forgive me for eavesdropping, but it sounds like the stolen book is of significance to the takeover."

I nodded, while I finished the divine pastry. "These are amazing Carrie. You have a real knack for baking. Have you always been able to create such heavenly treats?" I recalled her question. "The book is significant, in a way I've yet to determine. It's like the answer is just on the tip of my tongue, but I can't see it." I mixed my metaphors, but I was pretty sure she knew what I meant.

"Maybe you need another pastry." Dane quipped, as he reached for a second.

Carrie looked sideways at her brother. "Dane is practical so he doesn't like hearing this, but do you think there may be some mystical connection? Like the book is your clients good luck charm, or stronger, a talisman, without which his business will fail. And yes, I've always loved baking, but it was only with a life change recently that Dane convinced me to go into business with him."

"I'm sure Jane is all about practical steps too, not this woo woo witchy stuff you read in your books," Dane said affectionately, smiling at his sister.

"If only life was that black and white." I wasn't about to comment that not only did I know woo woo stuff to exist in the world, but that I was one of those unlucky enough to be touched by it. "Thanks for the ideas, I'm sure I'll get to the bottom of this mystery soon. Thanks for listening too, I appreciated the sounding boards, and your thoughts. Now, let's get this café set up. More people need to taste this awesomeness," I said, indicating the empty plate. With renewed energy I help manhandle the remaining pieces of furniture into place.

"I wonder if a spell to find lost things would locate the book?" Carrie mused dreamily, as she fluffed out some pale mint green tablecloths on each table.

"It might." I actually knew one and had used it before, many years ago. I couldn't believe I'd forgotten about that, but then I'd consciously tried to hide that side of me.

Chapter Eight

I realised brother and sister were watching me as my brain kicked into gear. Back into Freida mode properly, finally. After a day of fumbling around in the dark it finally felt like I was getting somewhere.

"Jane, are you okay?" Carrie asked. "Were the pastries too much?"

I shook my head, clearing my thoughts. "What? No, they were perfect. I was remembering how I solved a mystery for a previous client." I glanced at the wall behind the counter, noticing it's shiny wet blackboard paint. "Sometimes we have to put our faith in things we don't understand, like a prayer or a spell to find lost things." I grinned at the siblings. I wanted to run home and try that spell immediately, to see if it would locate the missing book. That would be rude, and I was enjoying helping Carrie and Dane set up their establishment.

"If you say so," Dane replied, raising an eyebrow as we moved the last table into place. "I'll stick with the practical, what I know, and of course coffee," he added with a grin. "I don't suppose you have time to help me grab all my tools from the van, before you run home and solve the mystery? I can bribe you with free coffee, tomorrow."

"Lead the way, no bribing necessary." I patted Dane on the back as I followed him outside. I nearly ran into his back as he stopped just outside the door.

Dane whispered something that I didn't quite hear, but it was enough to make me look around. The man with the distinctive leather shoes leant against the wall of the shop next to Carrie and Dane's not even pretending to look at his phone. He lifted his head a little, indicating for me to join him.

"Are you sure? Do you want me to come with you?" Dane muttered.

"I've got this." I whispered back. To the man I said, in a loud enough voice that he'd not mishear me. "I'm helping my friend now, either wait for me until I'm done, help, or go away." I hoped I sounded braver than my gurgling stomach. The stranger, half nodded, and remained where he stood, staring at the coffee cart. Ignoring him as best I could, I let Dane load my arms up with two plastic tubs of coffee cups, lids, spoons, sugars, syrups and assorted coffee condiments. Dane picked up the heavier of the two coffee making machines.

Inside he indicated that I put the tubs on the table closest to the counter. "We still have to finish the countertops." He indicated a blank spot to the left of the counter. "A brand new moveable counter will fit there, and some higher shelves on the far end and we should be open for business in a day or so."

Carrie hurried through and whispered something to Dane. Turning to me she added, "Jane, it was lovely to meet you, I hope I'll see you again soon. I have to run, I've an appointment I've forgotten about." She looked at Dane, "Don't forget that cart has to be empty, clean and gone by 5pm today."

"Yes Sis," he said to her back as she swung through the front door. "If you can help with a couple more loads, I'll finish cleaning the cart while you talk to your fan. That way I can make sure nothing happens to you." I could tell Dane had the same stubborn gene I had, so I didn't bother to protest. I carried the remaining few boxes and tubs into the building, while he brought in his coffee makers. At last the van was empty, except for the cleaning equipment. "When you are done with him, head home. I know you live close by, but I'll keep watch to make sure he doesn't try to follow you." I nodded, lost for words at the kindness of the barista.

I walked as boldly as I could, without trembling on the outside, invoking my protection from harm. With the invisible shield in place, I knew I'd come to no harm. One of my mentors, in the UK was both a private investigator and a practising shaman. Under his tutelage I began to understand that my ability to manipulate the elements wasn't necessarily a curse, as long as I could control it. I'd not thought of that part of my life for a while. It might be time to get back into the zone.

The man was a good head taller than I, still I managed to look him square in the eye as I asked, "Why are you following me? What do you want?"

"You are a friend of Brett Bently's." A statement, not a question.

I nodded curtly. He pulled his brow together, his bushy eyebrows forming a frown, his eyes squinting as he continued, "Stay away."

Did he know that Brett was currently thousands of metres in the air and so staying away from him wouldn't be a problem?

"I won't tell you again. Stay away from Mr Bently, from Bently Enterprises, or you'll regret it," the man said firmly.

"Why?" I challenged the man, though my legs were finding it difficult to keep me standing in an upright position.

Silence.

"I asked why," I persisted.

Silence. I gauged that having delivered the message I'd hear no more from him. Without looking back at Dane, I marched forcefully to my apartment building, up the stairs and through the front door. I refused to look back, knowing that Dane would keep his word and I wouldn't be followed. I exited through the stairwell, making it even harder for anyone entering the reception area to find my actual apartment.

By the time I'd locked my front door behind me I was panting like I'd run a marathon. Should I check to make sure Dane was okay? I didn't want the barista to get hurt if he attempted to protect me? I wished I'd thought to get his number, so I could text to check on him.

Grabbing a water bottle from my empty fridge, I remembered my plan to pick up some groceries. The view from my window didn't afford me oversight of the coffee van or the street below. I sipped my water slowly, forcing my heart to slow its pounding and my breathing to even out. *Far out brussell sprout, that wasn't fun.* But I didn't hate it. The adrenaline rush, reminded me of the reason why I loved the PI work. Dane and his sister were nice, so it wasn't a total waste of a day. I pulled up an online grocery store and placed an order that included fresh fruit and vegetables, cereal, yoghurt and pasta, as well as coffee, chocolate and fizzy drinks. The delivery guy would deliver to my door, as long as security were aware I'd placed an order. I didn't feel like venturing outside, so I rang down to the front desk and told them to expect a delivery later in the day. I probably should have told them about my tail, but felt silly mentioning it to them, they'd probably suggest I call the police.

My groceries wouldn't be delivered for an hour. I took my water, notepad, and laptop to my comfy lounge, using it like a daybed, with my legs stretched out along the seat cushions. A few seconds later I swung my legs over the edge. I couldn't sit, worrying about Dane. Was he okay? I sighed, grabbed my keys and my mobile and headed out.

The lift door dinged as I exited into the foyer. A sigh of relief escaped my lips, as there was no sign of leather shoes. *You can do this,* I told myself as I walked out into the afternoon sunshine.

Dane had his back to me, as he wiped down the outside of the van with a damp cloth. He swung around, as he heard me approach. "Jane! Is everything okay? The man waited at the bus stop, but I didn't see which bus he took, I was caught by a customer looking for coffee."

I couldn't help smiling at the concern on his face. "I'm fine, thanks, I was worried about you. I didn't have your number to check you were okay, so I came down to see. Plus I need to grab a couple of groceries," I fibbed, so he didn't think I came back just because I was worried about him.

Dane touched me briefly on the arm. My eyes held his gaze for what seemed like an eternity. Eventually, he broke the spell. "Do you have your phone?"

I handed him my mobile. He tapped a few buttons. "I sent me a text, from your phone. So we have each other's numbers," he smiled.

A large four-wheel drive pulled up beside us. The driver honked their horn. "I'm sorry Jane, this is the new owner of the van, I have to help him hook it up. Be careful." Dane looked like he wanted to hug me. I knew, because I felt the same.

"Sure, go do what you have to, we can talk later." I patted his arm as I turned towards the convenience store.

Just over ten minutes later I was back in my apartment. A couple of banana's in the fruit bowl, a drink of apple juice on the counter, and a muesli bar. My laptop open in front of me.

Who warned me off Brett and why?

Not Brett himself, or Kathy. Gerard? No, he was happy to tell me just enough not to be useful. That left Cody, Stanley, or someone else I'd not yet found. A yawn escaped my lips. I eyed the lounge. Should I grab a quick nap?

A banging at the door reminded me of my grocery order. Once all the items were tucked away in their allotted spots, I opted for a snooze on the lounge.

Sometime later I woke from a restless sleep where I'd been chased by strangers carrying leather briefcases. In my dream I'd invoked the spell to find the lost book. My head felt foggy, did I hear someone at the door?

No one stood outside when I cautiously opened the door. I checked my fridge, confirming I'd put my groceries away. Maybe a coffee would wake me up. Two scoops of coffee, and one of cocoa, for that extra sugar hit, and a splash of milk.

Before I could drink my concoction, my mobile phone beeped. I rummaged in my bag, A blocked number sent the words *You've been warned.*

True. The tall guy who'd been stalking me had warned me. Why did I need a reminder? It wasn't like I'd done anything since arriving home, except for ordering groceries and sleeping, restlessly. I sat back on the lounge, cringing as I bumped my legs on something hard. I lifted the cushion and peered underneath to find the problem. A small green book with a triquetra stared back at me.

Chapter Nine

I'd dreamt the locator spell, and upon waking, the book had arrived. I didn't remember that happening before. The threatening text message may have been from the person who'd been holding the book. Even so, how did they know my telephone number?

Brett had found my number, but then he owned a huge tech company. Gerard, Stanley, and Cody all had my number, courtesy of Brett. It wasn't the same number Gerard has used before. Stanely or Cody then? But still, something, didn't sit well. My sixth sense wasn't always on point, but as I had nothing else to go on, and I'd magicked the book to me, I decided to work with what I had.

I opened the book and started reading. The pages were old, yellowed, not parchment, but not of this century, or the last. The handwritten, flowery script, told the tale of a woman, one of Brett's ancestors. A healer during the time when women suspected of being witches were hung or drowned, she managed to live into her nineties, before mysteriously disappearing. The last few chapters of her book, were written by her daughter, gifted with similar traits her mother passed to her. A more practical woman, she shared some incantations, and recipes. A book meant to be passed down on the maternal side.

The last page listed eleven women, and Brett. "The book passed to Brett, because he was an only child," I muttered aloud. I flipped back to the recipes and incantations. Chicken broth for healing, a spell for protection, fruit cake for special occasions, a love spell, how to make a hearty stew, a spell for prosperity. The last line of this page caught my eye. *Warning – should this book fall into the wrong hands, any spells invoked will be reversed, so make sure you keep this safe, secret, and enjoy a long, happy and prosperous life.*

Did whoever stole this book know about the warning? Is that why the book was stolen, to send Brett broke? It didn't sound like something Stanley would do, he'd want to take over a successful company, not one that was failing.

Somewhere in the back of my brain, a lightbulb flashed. *What if...* I gently placed the book on my occasional table, on top of my book of crossword puzzles, which was the least dusty place I could think of. I tentatively patted the tome, mentally telling it, that everything was okay, it would be reunited with Brett soon. With my laptop in front of me I typed in *Carol Bently*, the name of Brett's ex-wife. I doubted she'd return to her maiden name; trading on her ex-husband millionaire's name was more her style.

It didn't take long to discover the latest on the woman who'd vowed to make my life miserable, when I'd revealed her multiple infidelities and fraud to her then husband. He'd paid her several million dollars to quietly agree to a divorce. I'd been surprised when she had conceded and disappeared without a fuss. "What happened Carol? Did you run out of money and attempt to coerce more from Brett? Did he refuse and you went after the book?"

I stared at Carol's smiling face at the opening of an art exhibition in the middle of London's Soho district. Dressed in a revealing little black dress, and sparkly jewellery, her arm was draped over the arm of the headline artist. Another photo of Carol, this time at a concert, standing smiling with the band. A third photo of the woman, dressed in a dark green pants suit, standing with Stanley Con. I gasped. I recognised his bald head and glasses, but even more so, I noted the resemblance between him and the man with the brown leather shoes. The same man stood behind him in the photo. The words underneath the photograph – *technological genius businessman Stanley Con planning to launch a ground breaking new company, with his son Otto, and his life partner of nine years Carol Means.* "So you did revert back to your maiden name," I whispered to the woman with the evil smile.

How could Brett not have known the connection? Because he's all about the business. He would have only vetted Stanley the businessman, the tech genius, not his private life.

The time on my laptop was 7:23pm. They'd be unreachable for hours yet. I knew from experience that a text message sent to someone in the middle of an overseas flight didn't always reach its destination. I opted for an email.

Brett, Kathy, hope your flight went well, and that the Kenny's are okay.

Carol is Stanley's partner; they are planning something soon.

Good news – I've found the book. I'll try to return to you asap.

Ring me as soon as you can.

I stretched, looking out the window at the high-rise buildings with lights blinking in their windows. I couldn't hear a lot of traffic noise, but I saw flashes of vehicles passing by on the street below. I drew my curtains closed and turned on all the lights in my apartment. Opening doors, and even cupboard to ensure no one was lurking inside, waiting to pounce. Assured that I was alone, I retraced my steps, checking the windows were locked, and that the front door lock was intact.

My stomach growled, reminding me to eat. I didn't feel up to cooking pasta. I took out a passionfruit yoghurt and scraped its contents into a dessert bowl. I opened the cereal box and shook a small amount on top of the dairy. I dropped a handful of blueberries on top. "A healthy dinner of sorts," I told myself.

While I ate my evening meal, I scrolled through all the information I could find on Carol and Stanely. Stanley's son Otto had some pretty serious links to organised crime in the UK, if the internet could be believed. He'd managed to avoid gaol time, thanks to his father's money.

Labels such as bank robber, drug dealer, and seriously injuring victims were attributed to him and the *Con Gang*, as his friends were dubbed. Another caption read *Pros and Cons*. Not people I wanted anything to do with.

If that message came from Carol, Stanley, or Otto and they knew roughly where I lived; did they suspect I was in possession of the Bently heirloom? I briefly considered packing a bag, getting on a bus, and heading north, or maybe west. That wouldn't solve anything. They find me, and I'd be no good to Brett if I were dead.

I sighed. As much as I didn't like it, my best bet was using my powers. I cringed at the thought. I'd no training or lessons in how my magical abilities worked. They'd caused more grief than anything else over the years. My parents never spoke about it, and back then, I didn't know the problems with electrical appliances and the weather were down to some dormant powers of mine. My fiancé dumped me, sighting my uncanny ability to break things, as the irreconcilable reason. I chose to travel, eventually joining law enforcement, learning a little about my powers along the way.

Calling the book to me in my dream state was a new one. Could I possibly send the book on to Brett's mansion? I'd been there before, but did that mean I could move the book across the world to arrive at the mansion before Brett finished his flight? The alternative would be to take a flight and deliver it in person, which may be a safer option. I didn't feel comfortable posting it to the UK.

On impulse, I looked up last minute flights. If I could make it to the airport by midnight, there was a chance I'd get on the flight leaving for the UK at 2am. It had a brief stopover, but I'd land in London only a few hours after Brett. My mind made up, I bought and downloaded my airline ticket.

I have a package for you. Will see you at the mansion soon.

I crossed out the message I'd planned to send to Brett, in case it got intercepted. Instead, I typed the words –

Remember how we solved the last puzzle.

Certain he'd remember and invoke the same protocol, briefly shutting down the company would, hopefully ensure its safety until I could return the book to its rightful owner. I hoped to plan how to stop Carol and Stanley, when I was safely in the air.

Chapter Ten

Rather than take my chances with buses and stalkers, I ordered a taxi. I packed a change of underwear, the little green book, and my passport, with my laptop in my backpack. With no plan other than to deliver the book to its rightful owner, I needed only my wallet, mobile, identity, and my laptop. I wasn't worried about money or my work deadlines. Brett had already transferred thousands of dollars into my account, *for expenses,* according to the notification.

As I exited the apartment building, I saw a light on in the shopfront that was soon to be Dane and Carrie's café. I felt guilty that I'd be away for the grand opening of *Macaroons and Mocha* according to the sign freshly painted above the door. I peered inside. Someone was behind the counter, Dane, probably, but I couldn't catch his eye. I scribbled a note on a page I pulled from my notepad and slid it under the door.

Sorry, had to go out of town on a job. Good luck with the opening. Jane
x

I texted the same message to his mobile number as I heard the sound of a car pull up beside me. The taxi light on the top assured me that unless the Cons or Carol had the ability to read my thoughts, or bugged my laptop, this was the car to take me to the airport. "Fair-weather, fare for the airport?" The driver leant over and swung open the passenger side door. "That backpack your only luggage?"

"Yes, thanks." I slipped into the front seat, looking around me for the first time since stepping foot outside. The knot in my stomach loosened as I couldn't see anyone lurking in the shadows.

"Heading out for work or pleasure?" The driver tried for amiable conversation as we progressed quickly through the streets towards the airport.

"Work, just an overnight thing." I decided on a harmless fib.

"International terminal, right?" The driver confirmed.

I realised my error, giving too much away, in case the driver was somehow part of the sinister plot, but I could be on my way to New Zealand or Singapore for a meeting. "That's right, thanks." I concentrated on my breathing, slow, deep breaths in and out, holding each one for a few seconds. This was real life, not a murder mystery. Even if Carol, or Stanley were trying to scare me, it didn't mean I was in danger. The food I'd consumed, only an hour ago, sat heavy in my stomach.

Even as a private eye I preferred to work from my desk, although that wasn't always possible. I remembered it was easier when I stayed in character as a private eye. I stressed less. Anxiety only took over when I focused on my fears. I closed my eyes, for a second. When I opened them again, I focused on the traffic on either side of the taxi. I took note of the buildings, apartment blocks, high rises, shopping centres, and industrial estates as they sped by my window.

Roads crisscrossed each other, with overpasses and underpasses, a tunnel that blacked everything out. I blinked a couple of times, until the glare of the streetlights and cars told me we were close. Signs pointing to the airport and the international terminal made it easy for the driver to find, though I suspected he'd taken multiple fares to and from the airport. "Here we are, the international terminal. Just go through those doors there and follow the signs," the driver said helpfully.

I scanned my card, paying the fare. "Thank you." I exited the car, and walked quickly to the glass doors, glad I'd remembered to grab my black cardigan as I quickly changed into my blue jeans and a fresh purple shirt. It was winter in the UK, but I'd deal with that after I landed and handed over the heirloom.

Feeling my agitation starting to rise again, I started my mantra – *I am safe, I am protected, I can do this.* The line up to check luggage wound around the bollards. I was thankful I only had to worry about my carry on. I removed my laptop, it's charger, and my mobile from my backpack, placing them in one tub, the bag in another as I passed through security. My guardian angel must have been beside me, because I passed through the security check without a problem.

I scanned my surroundings. I only had to wait a couple of hours for boarding, and saw no sign of Carol, Stanley, or Otto. I breathed a long sigh, relieved, as I expected to see either one of them waiting for me as I boarded. Sitting still wasn't an option, even in the comfy seats. I knew the time in the air would be close to twenty-four hours, maybe more. It would take all my will power to sit still for that length of time. I browsed the shops, where I could buy toys, cosmetics, clothes, books, magazines, chocolates, even the latest tech if I felt inclined. I could eat burgers, pizzas, chicken and chips, baked goods, the list went on. Drink choices included coffee, tea, milkshakes, smoothies, water, fizz, juice, spirits, wine or beer. I settled for a small bottle of water, a packet of dark chocolate coated raspberry lollies, a crossword magazine, and a book by an author I wanted to check out. *Why are books so expensive at airports – because everyone decides to buy books to read.* I answered my own question.

Window shopping, I'd only managed to while away thirty minutes. I found a seat away from other early passengers, where I could watch people coming and going. I sipped my water, grabbed a handful of lollies and opened the crossword puzzle. My fingers searched the front pocket of my bag, where I knew I'd stashed a few pens. Only fifteen minutes later I'd exhausted my guesses of the first puzzle, and I didn't want to cheat. My legs were restless, my intuition told me to get up and move. Tucking everything into my bag, ensuring I didn't damage the book, I headed to the toilet.

Paging Freida Everly. Freida Everly if you are in the terminal can you please identify yourself at the check in desk.

I hunched myself a little, wishing I'd worn my hoody. I was checked in as Jane Fairweather, and not Freida Everly. Stanley had been introduced to me as Freida. "It must be him, or his son, checking to see if I'm in the terminal." I didn't realise I spoke aloud until the group of teens wearing matching polo shirts and shorts with their team logo, edged away from me. The crazy woman who was talking to herself.

Could I stay in the toilet until they called for boarding? Not ideal. I'd murder a coffee, or some whiskey. No, I'd vowed off all alcohol for a while now. I slunk back towards the café, praying they hadn't bought a ticket so they could search for me. The licenced café offered all my favourites, but I stuck to a short black. Small amount of liquid before a long plane ride, but maximum kick. I never fell asleep on long trips. I was that one passenger with the light on reading or playing those games on the console on the back of the seats. Sometimes I'd choose a movie and watch it.

My sense of fight or flight, normally well developed, went into overdrive. I downed the coffee short in one gulp. Returning to the departure lounge, more passengers had begun to gather. Pretending to be engrossed in the puzzle in my book, my eyes darted from person to person, straining my ears to hear if they called for Freida Everly again.

If they did, I didn't hear it. I forced myself to sit still, and refrain from polishing off the whole packet of lollies. I did make one more trip to the ladies, as the flight called for the priority passengers. Boarding took so long, and I was cattle class, which meant I'd be amongst the last to enter the aeroplane. Finally, people sitting in rows toward the back were called and I joined everyone else as we slowly shuffled past the attendants. A swipe of our ticket and a smile. Padding along the corridor to the next door, where we showed our ticket and passed into the next, shorter corridor. Another smile, another flash of the ticket and a shuffle along the aisle past those already seated, until I found seat 73C. Thank goodness for an aisle seat. I tucked my backpack at my feet under the seat in front, rather than in the overhead locker. Less chance of things moving around or the book getting damaged if I could control it with my feet.

I fidgeted, wiggling in my seat to get comfortable, wishing I'd remembered to wear leggings instead of jeans for the long-haul flight. I tucked the little pillow under my arm, and the thick fluffy blanket into the pocket of the seat in front of me. Pulling my bag out, I extricated my puzzle mag, the book I wanted to read and my laptop, and shoved them into the pocket, with all the grace of an international globetrotter.

As my eyes adjusted to the lighting, I surveyed my surroundings as best I could. The window seat was occupied by an elderly lady who seemed to be already nodding off to sleep. The gap in between us hadn't yet been filled. Around me I could make out silhouettes. The young couple with the baby, the brothers and sisters traveling with their parents, older people, of all nationalities, but also quite a few spare seats. Maybe not everyone was keen to depart at 2am.

In the front section of the plane, I thought I caught a glimpse of someone I recognised. My breath caught in my throat. I couldn't place the person. Could it be the man with the leather shoes, Carol, Stanley, or just someone who looked familiar? I blinked and they were gone. Probably a trick of the light, or my overactive imagination. I couldn't change my situation now. If I stayed alert, nothing would happen to me or that book.

Chapter Eleven

Because I'd travelled before I knew the routine. The airline's generosity, a clever ploy to keep passengers' cosy and sleepy, included lots of small meals. I didn't bother walking for the first seven of the fourteen-hour flight to Dubai. When I couldn't distract my restless legs any longer, I walked a lap of the cabin, as recommended by health professionals, to limit the chances of deep vein thrombosis incidents. I normally wore my compression socks as an added precaution but they were tucked up at my apartment in my underwear drawer. Without staring too closely my eyes ran over the people I passed.

Families, individuals, couples, every combination I could think of, right in front of me. If Carol, Stanely, or Otto were on board, I couldn't find them. Nor could I pick out which passenger I thought I recognised.

I spent the rest of the flight reading, watching movies, playing on the game console, and eating the food as it was provided to me. The lady beside me stirred around the time the breakfast trays were delivered. "Excuse me dear, would you mind helping me with the table?" She asked in a crackly voice.

Mine sounded the same, considering we hadn't spoken to anyone for hours. I levelled her table out, locking it into place. Luckily for her, the person in front hadn't leant their seat all the way back. I copied the action with the table at the spare seat in between us. "Why don't you use this one too, if you need too. These tables aren't the biggest, and there's a lot of food and drinks on each of these trays." I handed her the tray that the hostess handed to me, helping the woman separate her coffee and juice into the spare table.

"Thank you dear. Even though I've flown every year for the last forty years, each time something has changed since my last flight." She sorted through the food items on her tray. "Where are you travelling to?"

"London, via Dubai." I answered, as I sifted through my own breakfast options. I smiled thank you at the hostess as she handed me an apple juice and a black coffee. I always managed to spill most of the little milks that were provided.

"We must be on the same flights," the lady said, a piece of buttered croissant posed near her lips. "I'm meeting my daughter at Dubai, and we are shopping there for a day or two."

I swallowed my mouthful of cereal. "My stopover in Dubai is only a couple of hours." I shuddered at the thought of spending any more than a couple of hours there. The airport terminal was huge, and I just knew I wouldn't enjoy spending any significant amount of time there. "I'm sure you'll have fun, spending time with your daughter." After eating, my new friend nodded off, leaving me to finish my crossword and start a new one. The movie wasn't catching me, and the console games were boring. I'd reached my limit of sitting still.

Dubai wasn't my favourite airport. Huge, flashy, and impersonal. Metal – gold, silver, platinum and lots of glass made up the exterior of the terminal from what I could tell. It took a long time to walk from the terminal where we left our first aeroplane, to the terminal where we to board the airliner to London. I walked with hundreds of other passengers, from my plane, the others that landed and those entering the airport – all heading towards departure gates. For a huge space there wasn't a lot of customer seating. Unless you wanted a meal, snack or drink at one of the many foodaries. Which I didn't. I kept my head down and followed the directions as best I could to the correct gate.

Security here was a little stricter. One pass through the guards on the way in from the aeroplane and another pass through on the way to the departing plane. Some people had to take off shoes, jackets, belts, hats and empty the contents of their carryon baggage for the guards. Lucky for me the guards were happy with just my mobile and laptop out. Signs around the staging area advised not to bring any liquid through. I remembered this from my last trip, deciding to wait for the next flight to have more water, and a coffee.

"The wait here seems to take longer than the rest of the journey," the lady sitting next to me said conversationally. I estimated we were similar in age. She sat next to a tall thin man with a blonde beard, nursing a tiny baby in his arms. "It's the first time we've travelled with Jasper. We're so lucky he's slept most of the time."

I felt a tug on my bag, tucked under my seat. Instinctively I grabbed my bag tucking it up on my lap. If the man sitting on the other side of me had tried to grab it, he was a great actor. About fifty years old with his nose in a book, an older lady lay her head on his shoulder. I twisted to see who sat behind me. I'd chosen this row because it sat so close to the wall where the stairs began that no one would be sitting behind me. I knew my cheeks were red, as adrenaline pumped through my veins. I couldn't afford for any stray energy to escape here. I opened the zip, checking for my valuables and the book. All of which appeared to be as I left them. I closed the zip and left the bag on my lap until we were called to start the boarding process.

My seat this time was a window seat. I didn't mind, as it appeared as with the previous flight there were only two of us in a row of three. "I hope you don't mind if I put my briefcase up on the spare seat after take-off," said the man with the short cropped black hair as he slid into the aisle seat. His suit was linen and crushed, and he had the air of a well-travelled business-man.

"That's fine by me." I responded, impressed he'd asked and not just spread his things out on the spare seat. We had eight hours until we landed, and I was exhausted. I knew I wouldn't sleep. Once, a long time ago, I'd tried to lie on the two seats together, but it was so uncomfortable, I'd never tried again. I refused to tip my seat back. Even when the passenger in front of me did so.

"Thank you. I have a deadline to meet by the time we land in London," the man said, as if that made a difference.

I remembered one of the editing jobs that had been passed to me just after Christmas. The author requested the job to be completed by midnight on New Year's Eve. "I do too, as it happens. I edit for a small publishing house." I added by way of explanation.

"I deal in antiques, and our firm is acquiring a particularly elusive manuscript said to date back hundreds of years." He stood, taking off his jacket, folding it neatly and placing it carefully on the seat between us. "The kicker is, it's supposed to be magic." He winked conspiratorially. I couldn't tell whether he was joking.

"Ah, all the best things are," I replied with what I hoped was the right mix of mystery and cynicism.

The man gave me a bemused look. "You don't know whether to believe me or not." He nodded sagely. "It's well documented that heirlooms and artefacts created with or imbued with, powerful magic, have made and broken kingdoms. Who are we to judge?"

Who indeed! I tried to get a glimpse of his face, to see whether he was winding me up, or serious. With his laptop on the table in front of him it was impossible to tell. He punched out a message on the keys, before tucking it and his briefcase under the seat in front for take-off.

Chapter Twelve

I must have closed my eyes for a few seconds, while the airline hostess, with the aid of the video in the console in the seat in front, prepared us for take-off. When I opened them, we were in the air. I panicked, a little disoriented. The screen in front of me confirmed I'd been asleep for less than five minutes. Still, I couldn't afford to nod off, with the heirloom tucked up in the backpack between my feet. I glanced around at the man one seat away and at the other passengers.

No one paid me any attention. I slowly release the breath I'd been holding. After the murkiness of the airport at Dubai I spent a few moments re-invigorating the shield of protection I'd invoked in the taxi. As I pulled out the puzzle book from my bag, my fingers confirmed Brett's artefact sat exactly where I'd left it.

My travelling companion was silent, tapping the keys on his keyboard. Tapping into my intuition I decided he wasn't a threat, and that his trade was a coincidence. Brett's heirloom wouldn't be the only magic artefact in the world.

We started our descent eight hours later. I was over tired, full to the brim with food, and raring to get out of the terminal and on the road to the mansion. The likelihood of snow when I stepped outside the terminal was high. I weighed up the time I'd waste finding a jacket, versus hopping in a cab and paying the fare to drive directly to the mansion.

I listened to the pilot advising that yes, it was snowing, and currently minus one degree outside. I needed a taxi, and a way of letting

Brett know I'd landed. In my haste to leave I hadn't organised a phone provider. I could turn on international roaming. It cost a lot, but I knew Brett would pay the bill if I needed him to. It'd be the easier option. "Do you have a thicker coat in your luggage?" The man in the linen suit asked as he pulled a thick woolly coat from his carry on.

"Nope. But I'm catching a taxi and going straight to my destination, so I'll be fine." I countered. "Do you mind if I ask, do you know how to turn international roaming on my mobile?" If he travelled as much as I thought he did, he might be able to help.

"It's easy. If you're with one of the major providers, all you have to do is turn on your mobile and accept the fees. You can turn it off again when you don't need it. The roaming doesn't need to stay on the whole time." He opened his mobile, which looked more like a mini tablet than anything else. "See, here." I watched as he turned his phone on and flicked through the screen. "This is still on aeroplane mode, but you get the idea."

"Thanks. Yes, that makes sense. I appreciate you showing me," I said earnestly.

As the pilot finished by saying we'd be landing within half an hour, I turned to pack my items into my backpack.

I didn't rush to stand. It always took a while for the aircraft crew to prepare for disembarking passengers. Watching the people in front head for the door, I didn't recognise anyone. The man from the seat near me had long gone before I headed out through the front door of the aircraft. "Thank you for choosing to fly our airline," the staff member, dressed immaculately in the company cream and red signature uniform smiled.

"Thank you for looking after everyone on the flight," I replied as I stepped through onto the metal corridor connecting the plane to the terminal. I progressed towards the baggage area, leading to the exit. I found myself in a crowd. Hundreds of people, walking in all directions, with luggage, chatting, talking, arguing, or with their heads down, focusing on their footsteps. I hefted my backpack onto my front, for better control, and kept my eyes firmly on the exit sign.

"Freida!" I recognised Brett's voice as I drew closer to the baggage rotunda. "I've a car outside, once you grab your luggage and get through customs."

"Brett! You didn't have to meet me, but a huge thank you for doing so. I've no luggage, only my carry on. I'm not even going to ask how you got through here, to meet me." I hugged my old friend, not even caring that he still called me Freida. He draped the coat he held in his arms around my shoulders. "Thanks, but won't you be cold?"

"I have three layers on; I brought this coat for you." He smiled. "I figured you'd be wearing Australian clothes."

"How are the Kenny's? Was anything stolen or damaged at the mansion?" I asked as we crossed the terminal to the exit. The air grew colder as we approached the sliding doors. I shivered.

"You can ask them yourself soon, and no," he added as he held open the door of the limousine waited just outside the doors, in an area normally reserved for dignitaries.

Brett and I strapped on seat belts as the driver moved the car away from the curb. The interior of the car was plush, black, leather. In the space between us in the back seat, sat a mini bar. Four different bottles of alcohol sat alongside a selection of tiny biscuits and nuts. "I've got a coffee waiting for you at the mansion," he assured me.

I reached into my backpack, balanced on my knee, and gently pulled out Brett's book. I handed it to him without a word. I scribbled a question on my notepad – *do you trust your driver? Could your car be bugged? Your computer? Phone too?* Brett's eyes grew wider at the next sentence I wrote. *I'm pretty sure Carol and Stanley are behind the whole thing. Danger - they have eyes on everything.*

Brett nodded. "The Kenny's are so looking forward to seeing you. That you made time to visit on your way to Germany, well, their chuffed." A master of the bluff, he'd taken to acting in high school and university.

"I'm so pleased it worked out this way. They've always been so friendly, and I have a day to spare before my conference." I played along.

Brett tapped the glass between the back seat and the driver. "Can we please make a stop at the next shopping centre?" The driver veered to the left lane, exiting at the next option. The road led up to the front of a large shopping complex. "I thought we'd spoil the Kenny's. These shops have the best sales, Mrs Kenny is always talking about it." He motioned for my pen and notepad. On it he wrote – *buying myself all new clothes, shoes, phone etc – why don't you buy yourself some new clothes, for the UK winter, and a bigger bag? My treat.* He grinned as I read his messy writing.

"Sounds perfect Brett! I know just the type of thing you mean. Let's meet at that café, the one with the sweet cupcakes we all love, in say half an hour?" On the paper I wrote – *with your new phone, can you alert the guards the company, and the police, that C and S are responsible …*

He nodded. "A great idea!"

I was nearly certain that Otto couldn't have bugged any of my gear, but just in case, I followed my own advice and replaced everything. My clothes were easily replaceable and held no sentimental value. I chose jeans, black leggings, a couple of purple shirts and a large black hoodie. I found a backpack, similar in style to the one I'd owned for years. On the way to the counter a cute purple suitcase with wheels caught my eye.

My laptop and mobile, I wasn't too keen to ditch. Brett would probably have a device that could debug electrical equipment. I found a gizmo at a tech shop that could block electrical signals. Whilst there, I picked up a second mobile, and a tablet.

I donated my empty backpack, and all the clothes I'd been wearing to the op shop at the entrance to the plaza. I wheeled the purple case containing my clothes, in front of me. Over my shoulder hung my new backpack,

The footsteps of the person behind me, I noticed by accident. As I stopped to look in a book shop window the clipped pace behind me stopped. As I pretended to check out the toys in the next shop, I heard the steps again. I clutched my bags tightly as I turned around. I recognised Otto Con immediately. I looked right through him, feigning ignorance. The sound his leather shoes made had given him away. Without hesitation I headed toward a security guard standing at the information counter.

"Excuse me, do you see that man, the one with the shiny leather shoes, the navy jeans and the thick leather jacket that sits just above the knees?" The guard looked over my shoulder and nodded. "He's been following me around the shopping centre. He tried barging his way into the change room in the ladies clothing section. I'm a little scared. Could you please tell me what my options are. I'm visiting from Australia, and I don't know what to do."

The kindly guard, frowned at Otto. "Don't worry about a thing madam. Leave it to me. Go and have a nice cup of tea and enjoy your stay." He strode towards Otto. I would've loved to see the look on his face, but I didn't dare turn around.

My heart pounded in my chest as I headed to Brett, seated at a table outside *The Sweet Treats.* I nodded towards where the guard stood, not letting Otto move. "Stanley's son has been following me." I filled Brett in on my last couple of days.

"I'd no idea I'd put you in harm's way Freida, er Jane." Brett sounded subdued, contrite, not emotions I'd have attributed to my eccentric billionaire friend.

"Do you have some gizmo to check our tech for bugs? I'd really don't want to throw out my mobile and my laptop." I leant forward, "and PS I don't mind, and you can call me Freida if you like." As I finished speaking, two people approached our table.

A waitress, dressed in a black skirt and white shirt placed a tray in front of us. "Two coffee chocolate thick shakes, and a plate of melting moments." She smiled.

A man, similar in age to myself, with thick glasses and a shock of dark brown spiky hair held out his hands. Brett handed him a shopping bag with his laptop, tablet, and mobile. I handed over my laptop and mobile. Pulling up a chair at a nearby table the man, dressed in a red and blue checked shirt, sat our technology in front of him. He grabbed a tool that looked like tweezers, and deftly pulled the back off each item. Once they were back in one piece, he typed a series of words onto the keyboard of each piece of equipment.

Within minutes he returned our technology. "All tracers are disabled, even the encrypted software, which is a prototype from Stanley's company."

"Thanks Boris. Please check over the office and the mansion. Take your team with you, and make sure it's all clean. Can you change the access codes for everyone except Stanley, and my ex-wife, in case by some chance she can still access the buildings."

"Sure, thing boss." He ambled back the way he'd come from.

As I took a bite of the most delicious melting moment, Brett's new phone rang. "That's great. Thanks for letting me know. I'll be there in an hour or so." He laid the phone on the table. "Police have picked up Stanley, Carol, and the rest of their team." Nodding towards the police that had handcuffed Otto. "My solicitor is drawing up the paperwork to make sure the company is safe, forever. As it happens, both Stanley and Otto returned on the same flight as you, Carol met them at Heathrow. I must go into work, to sign some documents, and meet with the heads of department." He paused, for long enough to eat a biscuit and drink some of his milkshake. "You have my driver, go to the mansion, see the Kenny's do some sightseeing, shopping, whatever you fancy."

A few steps from the table, Brett turned and returned to the table. He enveloped me in a huge hug. "Thank you, Jane, for everything. I can never repay you for all you did for me. My company is safe, because of you. I couldn't have done it without you."

Chapter Thirteen

If it wasn't for my mobile, assuring me it was 10am on January 6, I'd have been oblivious to anything other than I was too warm in my jacket. Jet lag was real. As I exited the taxi, I shrugged myself out of the beautiful purple fabric, tucking it on top of my new suitcase. The black shirt caught the heat, but I'd been having so much fun in London I'd not thought ahead to the weather upon returning home.

The doors to *Macaroons and Mocha* were open. The façade painted a soft, dusty pink, the enhanced the dark pink paint naming the new café. I dragged my now considerably fuller suitcase over the threshold. Having taken the opportunity of a few days shopping in London, I was very pleased to be home.

"Jane! Welcome back!" Dane bounded out from behind the counter, covering the area between us in a couple of steps. "I was so worried about you, when I found the note and the text that night before we opened. My sister told me not to worry, but still...I couldn't help it."

I'm so sorry, I meant to text you when I landed, but I got caught up." I wanted to hug my barista friend. Apart from Brett, Kathy, and the Kennys who expressed similar relief that I'd solved their mystery without personal damage; it'd been a long time since anyone had expressed concern for my wellbeing. A fuzzy tingle of gratitude wound its way over my shoulders. "I'm so sorry I caused you to worry."

"See, I told you there was nothing to worry about." Carrie smiled as she entered the room from the kitchen. "Jane, welcome back, you look exhausted, let us get you something on the house. Dane, let the poor woman sit down before she falls."

"I'm so sorry I missed the opening." My body thanked me as I sat, even though I'd been cooped up in an aeroplane for over twenty-four hours, sitting in a space with light and leg room was totally different. I lay my jacket on the back of the chair next to me and unzipped my suitcase. As Dane and Carrie arrived at my table with a plate of macaroons and what looked like an iced mocha, I placed a teapot with the union jack emblazoned on it, a little bear with a red hat and blue coat, a clock tower and a red telephone booth onto the table. "I found these, I thought they'd look great on a display shelf in the café. Presents to celebrate your opening."

"Oh Jane, they're perfect! You shouldn't have, though, thank you so much." Carrie leant in and hugged me.

Dane eyed the items on the table. "You were in London? For what, a whole two days?"

"Something like that, I admit most of the time was spent in the aeroplane. Still, snowing in London, that sight never gets boring." I grinned.

"One day," Carrie sighed wistfully. "So, tell us, does that mean you solved the mystery?"

"Yes, I did. You were right Carrie, the book was the key, and it is magic." I couldn't help smiling at the look on Dane's face.

"Well, as long as no one got hurt." Dane said. At that moment, a stream of customers entered the café. Dane and Carrie returned to the counter.

I nibbled on the macaroons, each bite creating an explosion of sugar with a touch of peppermint, orange, and in the case of the pink, strawberry. The mocha contained just the right balance of bitter coffee and sweet chocolate. A yawned escaped, between mouthfuls of deliciousness. I longed for my own bed but knew the best cure for jetlag was to stay awake until my normal bedtime. As the line at the counter thinned out, I handed my empty plate and glass to Carrie. "I'm going to get changed into more appropriate clothes for the weather, and I might go for a walk, to stretch, and keep myself awake. I'll call in later."

"We've glad that you are back." Carrie smiled.

"Ditto," Dane mumbled from behind the noise of the coffee machine.

I chose the lift, though my bag wasn't heavy I didn't fancy dragging it up the three flights of stairs. On top of my mail, on the table outside my door, was a note to check in with the security staff at reception. They could wait, until I'd showered and changed.

On second thoughts...It looked as if a tornado had swept through my apartment. My clothes, books and the contents of my kitchen cupboards were strewn across the floor. I considered just tidying it all up, but decided against it. I walked through the rooms, assessing the damage and confirming no one was lying in wait for me. I left my suitcase just inside the door, locked it and ran the three flights down to reception.

"My apologies Miss Fairweather, we tried to contact you on your mobile number for days. With no answer at all we've had no choice but to end your lease early." The broad-shouldered tall guard frowned. "It's not my decision you understand. We received multiple reports of disturbances in your apartment. When we couldn't contact you, we opened the door to make sure you weren't injured. The place was a mess. The manager called the police. We weren't sure whether to be worried about your safety or send police out looking to arrest you."

"What did you decide?" My brain, still trying to process the events, switched into sarcasm mode. "I'm here, safe, the victim of a break and enter. Should I be concerned I'll be arrested? Do I have a day to vacate my apartment, should I leave now, and without taking any of my belongings."

The guard raised his eyebrows. "I don't make the rules." He countered sternly. He handed me a piece of paper. An eviction notice, giving me seven days to vacate the property. Dated six days ago.

"Tomorrow – really? Can you confirm I won't be arrested if I stay here tonight?" Even I was surprised at the level of sarcasm in my voice.

He nodded curtly, I knew I was pushing his buttons, but I just didn't care.

"Right then, I'd better get going. Do I need to call the police, about the break in?" I held up my phone, ready to dial the number.

The guard picked up the handset for the landline. "Don't bother, they've already assessed the scene. I doubt they'll want to speak to you."

Without another word, I turned and marched back up the stairs. London time was twelve hours behind, give or take, but I knew Brett would be awake.

"Jane, I take it you arrived home without a problem. I wanted to thank you again for your help," the familiar voice beamed at me from across the world.

"Until I arrived, yes. Stanley must've sent someone to ransack my place, to search for your book, while I was on my way to the airport. The owners of the apartment have decided to evict me, when they couldn't find me, they thought I'd skipped town." I forced my tone to soften; it wasn't Brett's fault.

"Come back here. I'll take you on as head of my security." I could tell by his tone, that it was a serious offer.

"Thank you, and I may do that, eventually. Before I decide, I think I want to see more of this country."

"If you need anything, I'm here, any time of the day or night. I've deposited a thank you, in your account for saving my company and my family. The book is back where it belongs, at home. I took your advice, no one will be able to hurt the Bently name again. Thank you Jane and take care. Let me know what you decide." My knees wobbled a little as I checked my bank. Sparks flew from my fingertips as I made my way to the lounge to sit. I didn't bother to keep my energy in check. As much as I liked Dane and Carrie, I was over the big city, the private eye work, the danger. I loved it, but it was time for a change. I might return, one day, but for now, the open roads of this big country beckoned.

The End

Sarah Lewin

If you want to know more about me or my books, here are some details. Alternatively, please make contact via any of the social media listed below:

Email: sarahlewin@sarahlewin.com.au   or   sarahlewin_author@gmail.com

You Tube: https://youtube.com/@sarahlewinangelwisdom539

Blog: https://sarahlewin.com

Facebook: https://www.facebook.com/SarahLewinAuthorWitchyMysteryBooks

Instagram: https://www.instagram.com/sarahlewin_author/

Amazon: https://amazon.com/author/sarahlewin

Goodreads: https://www.goodreads.com/author/show/43342156.Sarah_Lewin

Book Bub: https://www.bookbub.com/authors/sarah-lewin

My Witchy Mystery Books:

Witch Wisdom Series:

#1 – *Crone Wisdom*

#2 – *Ancient Wisdom*

#3 – *The Wisdom of the Witches*

There are two free novellas in this series

The Coven

Kai's Story

Spirit Town Cozy Mysteries:

#1 – *Autumn Leaves Are Falling*

#2 – *Secrets Ghosts and Whispers*

#3 – *The Ghosts of Spirit Town*

Novella

Beth's Return

Misty Vale Cozy Mysteries:

#1 – *A Very Crafty Christmas*

Novella
Coffee Mystery and Magic
Stand Alone Books
Broken Lies
Anthologies
Tales of the Lost Things
I also have a range of children's books available, and some more cozy mysteries due for release in 2025

www.ingramcontent.com/pod-product-compliance
Lightning Source LLC
Chambersburg PA
CBHW071314200626
46813CB00015B/2202